also by Bo Carpelan
in English translation
BOW ISLAND

Dolphins in the City

BO CARPELAN

Translated from the Swedish by
SHEILA LA FARGE

A Merloyd Lawrence Book
DELACORTE PRESS/SEYMOUR LAWRENCE

Originally published in Swedish
under the title *Paradiset* by
Albert Bonniers Förlag, Stockholm

**Library of Congress
Cataloging in Publication Data**

Carpelan, Bo Gustaf Bertelsson, 1926–
Dolphins in the city.
Translation of Paradiset.
"A Merloyd Lawrence book."
SUMMARY: A fourteen-year-old Finnish boy
experiences both pain and pleasure in
his relationship with a retarded friend who
possesses some rare insights.
[1. Mentally handicapped—Fiction.
2. Finland—
Fiction] I. Title.
PZ7.C223Do3   [Fic]   75-8001
ISBN 0-440-05073-1

Contents

It's called Paradise because it's no paradise at all. Because if everything were nice and easy we'd be bored to death and never learn a thing. It's called Paradise because it's the only place where we can feel at home and live and face our troubles. That's why it's called Paradise, because it isn't one at all.

—Otto Söder

Good-bye to Bow Island

When they left Bow Island it was a dull September day with low, scurrying clouds. Steering the last load over the gray ocean toward Söder's dock, they had to ease off the sheet and luff along so as not to soak the brown paper bag and the white duffel full of bedclothes. Nora had already helped them bring over most of their things, now Gerda and Marvin came themselves, with Marvin's boat, which he held onto like something precious and fragile. He sat with his back to Bow Island all the way, scarcely even glancing behind him. It was as if he had moved away long before. He had spent the summer making the three-masted ship model with Söder's help.

Nora was down at the landing to meet them. Gerda swung the boat up into the wind and alongside the pier. Wind wore away into the pines; the birches stood flecked with gold against the blue-gray sky. There was a smell of autumn in the air. Nora steadied the boat so that it wouldn't slam against the pier. Söder walked slowly down to the shore, as fast as he could with his bad heart. Bow Island lay shrouded by a fine misty rain, but through the clouds, the autumn sun suddenly shone forth on the cliffs and grass as if wanting to remind them how beautiful it could be there, how fragrantly green the summer had been. After they had unloaded everything, Marvin was still sitting in the boat.

"Up you get, lazybones!" shouted Nora. "First hand me your boat, so it won't get wrecked before it's properly launched."

She knelt down and offered him her hand. Marvin grabbed it but wouldn't let go of his boat. Deftly and swiftly he vaulted ashore. He didn't look around, but walked right over to the blue van where the driver sat smoking. There were the four chairs, the cabinet, the basket holding kitchen utensils, and the gate-legged table. The beds had already been moved.

Dad had managed to get them a one-room apartment with a kitchen, off the entry leading to the inner court of our building. Gerda was to start a job cleaning in a factory. We hoped that Marvin would be able to hold down a job, too, so that he could contribute a little to their very meager funds. But they had left Bow Island for good. It was to be sold off gradually by its owners, divided up into small lots, filled with summer visitors, with summer cottages, summer docks, and summer pleasure boats. Gerda stopped and gazed out toward the familiar gray-black wooded rise, with its golden rim of birches by the shore and along the path to their home, now damp and cold. Damp it always was, but it had been their home.

Söder invited them in for coffee. The driver heaved himself out of his car reluctantly. Marvin kept silent and everything felt heavy.

"Anyway, what a blessing we'll be living on Sea Street. The name sort of feels like home," said Gerda. "And the place is cozy, though of course it's dark."

Outside the windows the trees lashed about violently.

"Well, Gerda, we really wish you luck with your job in the city, and should you ever feel lonely, remember we're right here," said Söder.

"Rrroaaaa, rrroaaaa!" screeched the parrot crossly from his cage in the dusky corner. Marvin raised his head.

"I didn't row," he said. "I didn't want to. He can scold all he likes."

"Right," said Söder.

"It's no good if it's stormy. The dolphins can help— they carried Dad away. But now there aren't any."

The driver fidgeted on his chair, cleared his throat and announced, "We should be off now."

"Yes," agreed Gerda. "And in the city we'll find Johan and friendly people to help us the way you have here."

She smoothed her hands over her apron, loosened the bow at her back, took off the apron, and folded it into the string bag that Marvin had knotted when he was still very young. But Nora leaned her wise owl face with her big glasses toward Marvin and said, "Come along. I have something to say to you."

Holding his boat with his right hand, and taking Nora's hand in his left, Marvin walked out onto the windy open space outside the front door. Dusk was beginning to fall.

"Listen. You feel sad and empty just now, but we all have to, once in a while. Otherwise we couldn't feel good the rest of the time," said Nora. "Do you understand, Marvin?"

She saw his face crumple with effort. His underlip pouted. He shook his head.

Nora dug her hand into the pocket of her jeans, drew out a stone which looked bright in the gray twilight. It was oval like an egg, and she handed it to Marvin.

"Feel this. Hold it in your hand, not too tightly and not too loosely. Whenever anything feels heavy to you, then try to put it into this stone. That way you'll be able to bear the heaviness and hold it in your hand. There are whole mountains from around here in this stone."

"Are the dolphins there? They carry me when I'm scared and drowning."

"They're there, too. But they are invisible."

Marvin held up the stone as if he wanted to see through it. Then he stuffed it into his pocket. "That's good. It'll help. But it's not like you."

"No, it isn't," Nora answered. "I'm the only one who looks like me. At least, almost the only one. Elsa Stenström has nearly the same nose."

"That stuffed owl on the cupboard looks like you," said Marvin. "Don't let them stuff you."

"Not for a while yet," answered Nora. "Don't lose the stone. And I'll come visit you soon on Sea Street."

"Here," said Marvin. He handed her his ship model. "The stone is for me. This is for you."

"No," Nora answered in a soft, quiet voice. "You should give that to Johan, from you and me and all of us here. Promise?"

She looked up into his face, which was wet with rain. Rain dripped from his lips, and she took out her handkerchief and wiped his mouth. Wind lashed into the trees, a tremendous, heavy wind full of autumn, smelling of earth and sea.

"The owl looks like you," Marvin said.

He turned and walked off toward the van. The driver already had the motor running. Nora stopped, dashed past Söder and Gerda, and reappeared carrying the stuffed owl. Its wide-open eyes, glassy with horror, stared out through the autumn evening, at the car all loaded up, and at Marvin's face with his blond hair and small, close-set eyes, capable of shining so suddenly, so brightly. His whole face glowed with joy. Nora handed him the owl, and he took it.

"But we really can't accept that," protested Gerda.

"It looks like me," said Nora. "Marvin wants you to have it along in town. And it's important to exchange gifts. This is like me, stuffed. Isn't it, Marvin?"

Marvin nodded his head vigorously. All Gerda could do was laugh. She hugged Nora, shook Söder's hand. There was not much left to be said. She climbed into the front seat next to Marvin. Then the car started with an angry roar. It careened along the winding forest road. The owl stared out of the window with its large, bright, astonished eyes; but there was something guarded about its expression. Then Söder's cottage and Paradise disappeared among the dark trees. Later, from the head of the inlet, they caught another glimpse of it and of Bow Island, a dark contour against the gray, wind-whipped water. They both sat in silence.

The Courtyard

Daylight was failing but the sky was clear when the car swung in through the entry and across the courtyard, while I ran alongside. Mrs. Berglund screamed in her whiskey tenor to Peter, who was knocking a football around the yard, "Here they come!" Then Peter kicked the ball up and at the garage door, making it thunder like a cannon. Peter was all limbs and elbows, quick on his feet, eyes like a weasel, hair like dandelion down. He positioned himself for a good stare.

I'd been waiting almost an hour out on the street and seen the windows in the houses light up, one by one. People came home from work, dogs barked, and everything was a little unreal. Gerda and Marvin were coming. It was as if a piece of my summers was about to root itself firmly in the asphalt and among the paving stones, the stairs, and the dark rooms. How would it turn out? Almost like an answer, the sun slid out from behind the rain-swollen clouds and shone on the spire of the Russian church far away at the end of Sea Street, which was like a long cleft in the city. Gulls rose silently into the wind and swept out again toward the ocean, like white scraps of paper. I felt both excited and anxious. I remembered how we had sat over Gerda's letter at home, the letter in which she told us that the property on Bow Island was to be sold and that they were having a hard time, that she knew people in the city who could arrange a job for her and could we perhaps help her find a place to live? It seemed quite hopeless, but when the old janitor's apartment became available, Dad had a talk with the manager. The manager came from the islands, too; he'd moved into the city once long ago himself. When he came over one evening, he shook his head, saying,

"They'll have a hard time. Very hard."

"But she's strong and a good worker and she's been promised a job. They can't go on out there, all alone."

"Well, of course they can have the apartment. But it's not cheerful. It's dark most of the day."

"There's really no choice. The rent is very reasonable. Also perhaps we can help them if they're living nearby."

"I remember how difficult it was for us. We didn't get much help, either. We went around for many years scarcely knowing a soul. And since I was a boy, I had to fight a lot to get accepted. What's he like, Marvin?"

We told him about Marvin, how good he was with his hands, how difficult he could be when a fixed idea got hold of him, how important it was to treat him just like the rest of us; how he shouldn't be pampered or threatened, or given a hard time.

"Like walking on thin ice," said the manager. "You'd better have a talk with the others around the court, Johan. So he won't get into trouble."

I thought of Peter's tough fists and his gang. I felt fear in my stomach. I had a few friends, school friends, but they didn't live here. Here, I walked across the courtyard alone and no one came over to me yet, even though they might shout after me, "Mommy's boy!" or "Think you're something special?" I tried not to provoke them. I avoided talking with them. I had my own room and my own view out over the black metal roofs.

I had wanted the yard to be empty when they arrived. All loads of furniture look strange and naked. Kids gathered around, attracted by curiosity, from every corner of the court.

"What weird baskets!"

"And what a table!"

"They're from the country."

"They sure look it."

Gerda opened the door and got out. I noticed that she was wearing her good clothes. But Marvin didn't want to leave the car. Gerda took my hand. "Thank God you met us. How are your mom and dad?"

The kids listened with interest. My ears turned red. "Fine. They're still at work. How's Marvin?"

"He hasn't said a word the whole way here."

"Hi, Marvin!" I called to him. "Now you're here. Come on out! Shall I help you?"

I heard my own voice. It sounded like a magpie wounded in the wing. I saw Marvin sitting there, pale in the face, holding his boat in one hand and the owl from Nora in the other. I would gladly have exchanged the owl for Nora. She always knew what to say and do. I was a mass of indecision. The driver slammed the door, opened the back of the car, and started lifting out baskets, suitcases, the few simple pieces of furniture. Marvin looked at me, shifted himself slowly out of the car. I grabbed his arm. He stood still, looked around: walls, the staring kids, the deepening autumn sky over the balconies where carpets were hung out to air.

"Hi, do you play football?" shouted Peter.

Marvin shook his head, swinging it vehemently from side to side. But Gerda said, "We're the Lundgrens. This is Marvin and I'm Gerda. I hope we'll get along and that you'll play nicely with Marvin and help him. Though he's big, he's more like you, because he's been very ill—I'm sure Johan has told you about that."

I said nothing. I walked around the car to help unload it. I didn't hear a word from the kids; Peter was silent, too. I wanted to be invisible. I couldn't cope. Someone shouted, "Have you ever seen such a radio!"

I picked up the old 1930s radio that had been standing on a table and carried it off toward the dark entry, through the open door, and into the room with its worn-out linoleum floor and the harsh light, still without a shade. We had been in there to wash the windows and clean up. Dad had seen to it that the electricity was working, Mom had washed the floor, and I had tried to clean the gas stove. It was old and rusty. I set the radio down on the windowsill and walked out again. I met the driver, who was carrying two chairs. Gerda came with a basket, and said in passing, "Take Marvin's things so he can help you." I went out to where Marvin was still standing by the car door.

"Is that really your name, Marvelous Marvin?" said a little girl, staring up at Marvin. "How did you get such a silly name?"

"His name is Marvin," I said. "And that's a good name. Come on, Marvin, let's put your things away, and then we can both help unpack the rest."

"What a jerk!" Peter shouted loudly, bouncing his football on the car roof. I led Marvin through the entry, felt the football pound into my back. I turned, left Marvin. The whole courtyard trembled; anger like tiny red dots swam before my eyes. I went over to Peter and his sneer. I said, "Look out! He's not well, and if you get him angry . . ."

"Then what . . . ?" said Peter, stepping closer. He pulled me to him, pressed his hand against my face, and pushed me backward. He was chewing gum.

I saw his face close to mine and struck at it, blindly. It was like hitting a thin stone mallet. Momentarily, gasping for breath, I grabbed hold of his neck. We stood weaving like two drunks, until someone came and separated us.

"Now what's happening just when we're moving in?"

Gerda studied us intently, holding us apart. She was strong. She said,

"This is no way to welcome us. Marvin will be frightened if he sees you. It wasn't his fault that he was injured when he was born. What's your name?"

"Yeah," said Peter.

"Not much of a name. Well, try to keep the peace. What Marvin needs is help. How about it?"

She left us abruptly. Peter stood still, then spat to one side, turned, and sauntered off.

In a very low voice I said, "He's mean. I couldn't hold back, he got to me."

"We can work it out later," said Gerda. "Now come help Marvin feel at home."

I grabbed two suitcases and started dragging them toward the door. Marvin sat on a chair in the chilly room. He was facing the window—a narrow slit opening onto a wall. He'd arranged the owl and the ship model in front of him. He was chewing a bite of a cheese sandwich. The room began to fill up with their things. The two beds we had moved in for them were cluttered with cardboard cartons of various sizes.

I said, "You'll see, the owl will like living here."

Marvin studied it. He said, "It's Nora's. She'll get it back. But it's okay. It can see in the dark. And it's dark here."

"But there'll be light. You have electricity now, and you can have lots of lamps. You couldn't on Bow Island."

I shouldn't have mentioned that name. Marvin cradled his head in his arms on the windowsill. He didn't answer. A hard wind blew in through the entry, and the door banged. Gerda and the driver passed each other on their way to and from the car. I said,

"We could help them, Marvin."

Marvin didn't answer.

Gerda came over, rested her hand on the nape of Marvin's neck, and said, "You can smell the sea out there, Marvin. It's not far away. And you can have the alcove in the kitchen for yourself. There's room for a bed, you'll see, and a table. Room for all your things in the cupboard at the foot of the bed. It'll be your own room. You can do anything you want with it. Just you. No one else."

Marvin sat up and asked, "No one else?"

"No one."

"The owl can see in the dark. If you can see in the dark, you're all right."

"That's true."

"Okay, then. I'm coming."

Now he was completely calm. He got up and we walked together back to the car. Almost everything had already been brought in, only the heavy cabinet was left. Marvin walked over to it, squatted down, closed his arms around it.

"You can't handle that," a little boy shouted.

Slowly, Marvin lifted the cabinet. He teetered slightly, I felt fear like a cold trickle of water down my spine: What if he fails, or falls? He steadied himself, turned slowly toward the entry with the cabinet in his arms. The kids moved aside. There was complete silence. Dusk was falling swiftly now, soon it would be difficult to see clearly at all. Someone turned on the courtyard light. I lifted the little palm tree potted in the wooden keg and followed Marvin. Gerda had got out a cloth for the table, a shade for the lamp; light suffused the room like a warming sun. The newly washed rag rugs brightened the floor. Sweat had come out on Marvin's forehead. He slowly lowered the cabinet against the wall. He got up and listened. Out in the court some sea gulls were still calling out, shrill and resonant.

"Gulls! Just like at home!"

"We *are* home now," said Gerda.

"They'll freeze soon," said Marvin. "Soon the snow will come and they'll freeze. Then I'll warm them and they'll live again. I'll bring them in here where it's warm."

He nodded to us, his hair falling over his forehead. His face shone with delight.

The Alfreds

A beer-bottle cap lay at the bottom of the Alfred family's swimming pool. It glared up at us like the remains of some strange fish. Looking down at the green tiles, Mrs. Alfred said, "Something wrong with the cleaning system. Nothing works in this house."

"It sure is big," said Dad, suddenly turning red in the face.

"A toast," announced Mr. Alfred. "And welcome to our humble abode."

The humble abode consisted of a two-story house with six rooms and a den. Then there was the swimming pool plus a sauna and a two-car garage. Bright net curtains hung in the picture windows, richly patterned like the underskirts of a folk dancer. The open fireplace was large enough to roast a whole wild boar.

"Now they'll get drunk," said Erik. "Let's split."

We split. Past the sauna, the bar, the den, the TV nook with its enormous sofa. Upstairs to the chrome-shiny hall with its orange-colored carpet and into

Erik's room. This was decorated in green and white, and behind the large, gleaming windows I could guess at the dark contours of pine treetops. Erik turned on the stereo, then looked me over.

"You've shrunk."

"I've grown two inches. Soon I'll be as tall as Marvin."

"Oh, him. How's our little summer idiot? Excuse me, but you have to face facts. I do some stupid things myself, but it's equally stupid to pretend that he's normal. Isn't it?"

"Just who do you think is normal?"

"Isn't that question itself a little crazy? There's nothing wrong with Marvin, except what's wrong with him. Cigarette?"

I shook my head. "Sometimes he's even smarter than you or me."

We were both quiet for a while. Then Erik said,

"They say Dad's business is going to hell. That's why they're carrying on this way now."

I had nothing to add. I wandered around his room, looking at all his stuff: tape recorder, movie camera, model trains, the microscope. I leaned over that. I'd always dreamed of having a really good, big microscope. Erik adjusted it: "Can you see now?"

I peered into a world that might have been an ocean in which unknown creatures swam about in their own shimmering green light. Everything in that world was completely silent and beautiful; no one drank, no one quarreled, no one shouted. There was no distress there, only the signs that I couldn't understand, shapes that my eyes couldn't make out; the whole world was full of them. It was like floating face down in crystal-clear water with your eyes open.

"Do you think Marvin might be interested in coming over here?" Erik asked. "But if he got violent or smashed something, then of course there'd be a real scene."

I barely heard what he was saying. Reluctantly, I pulled myself away from the microscope. "If he's with calm people, he's calm, too, most of the time."

Erik wandered nervously around his room. He said, "We aren't calm people. If someone lets a match fall or spills a drop, Mom comes running with a rag. And Dad goes on and on about long-haired radicals and politics and taxes and how he has slaved and sweated at work and this is all the thanks he gets. Do you quarrel at home?"

"Hardly ever."

"How do they live, Marvin and his mother?"

"In one room with a kitchen alcove. Marvin lives in the alcove. It's quite dark, all day."

"How can people live in rat holes like that?"

"They have no choice."

I heard Dad's voice raised to falsetto, followed by a resounding volley of laughter. Erik said,

"If this balloon bursts, we'll all end up quite soon in one room with a kitchen alcove. Dad will get work as a plumber, and Mom'll have to start cleaning. She's good at that. Beatrice will go soft in the head. And I'll run away."

"Where to?"

"South. The Bahamas—you can earn good money there. Become a frogman, dive for pearls. I got a frogman's suit for my birthday. Underwater, you don't have to see all the phony humans and you can't hear their dumb talk. And it's clear all the way to the bottom."

"And silent."

"And silent."

We smiled at each other; we shared the same opinion. I suddenly was aware that there was something I liked about Erik, in spite of his bragging, in spite of the fact that he acted superior and was often nasty. He always said what he thought. It was strange, but I could easily picture him in Marvin's kitchen alcove, with the mini night table and the cupboard at the foot of the bed. There, in any case, he wouldn't be able to pace back and forth like a caged animal.

He turned off the stereo, the TV. The light in the microscope went off by itself. He said, "Sometimes I don't want to own any junk at all. Just live clean as a whistle. Know what I mean?"

I nodded.

"Sometimes Mom tells me about what her life was like before. Her father started from scratch. They were poor. They had a hellish time, and I suspect Marvin has quite a hellish time, too, if he could realize it."

"Sure he can, sometimes."

Dad was standing in the doorway, his hair neat, his gaze a little glassy. His wrinkles looked deep, and he was holding a glass. I understood, all at once.

"Well, what are you young men up to?"

"Letting our hair grow, talking about sex," Erik answered. "Now and then, smoking and drinking."

"Oh, come on, we're sitting here talking," I said. "About everything."

"Come back here!" shrieked Erik's mom from the living room, where the stereo started whipping up South American dance music with a chorus of husky voices. Dad disappeared. Erik rooted around in his desk drawer and took out a photograph.

"Where did you get that?" I asked.

"From Nora."

We looked at the print: Midsummer Eve on the island, all of us lined up for Nora's box camera— Söder, Dad and Mom, Marvin, myself. That beautiful, mild Midsummer Eve a thousand years ago when Erik and Beatrice turned up and shattered it.

"You're not in the picture," I said.

"On the whole we should never have come," said Erik. "Well, there's always room for improvement, as the man said, sentenced to death."

I didn't understand him. I scarcely understood myself. I saw the two of us reflected in the dark windowpanes: two totally unknown boys. I often didn't understand Dad and Mom at all, either. I realized that the things I had discussed with them last summer, I couldn't discuss with them now, nor did I want to. I had started talking to myself. That summer, that midsummer, was incredibly remote. I remembered how angry I had become, how I had run away. And now? Was I so very different now? Didn't I basically avoid anything that was difficult as best I could? Then I thought of Marvin standing there by the car door, with his ship model and his stuffed owl. I remembered Gerda's face, not accusing, but not happy, either. I studied myself standing beside Marvin in the photo. It had been a hot summer. We lived out on Pine Point. Perhaps now, at this very moment, Nora and Söder were sitting by their little window overlooking the inlet, Nora reading aloud from one of her favorite storybooks. What had she once said about stories? That they were truer than most anything else. In the photograph she was standing with her hand raised, laughing.

An ambulance sped past with its siren howling, down the parkway, driving a hole into the silence, into the music, disappearing like an echo.

Marvin was holding a bouquet of flowers. I didn't remember that. He had looked right into the camera; nothing had changed, he would never change, always stay the same, always be a child, his whole life. I wondered if he didn't want to be an adult. I wondered whether he ever dreamed of becoming someone else. Would you be happier, then, if you grew up and became someone else, if you changed and maybe couldn't recognize yourself any more?

The candle flames flickered in a draft. Erik leaned toward me. "If I hit the road, would you come along?"

"What about money?"

"Oh, money, that'll work out. I have a bank account."

"I didn't know."

"You don't know much."

"Maybe. But there's really no reason I should."

We sat in silence. I noticed how pale Erik looked. He said to himself, "Erik Alfred, the man who knows everything, who can do everything, sees everything."

"And has everything!"

"Has everything!"

Erik looked at me with his face like a mask. He drew his mouth into a smile. I couldn't answer him. I suddenly had a powerful longing to get away from that house; I longed for home. Down in the living room, the music abruptly started again on a note high enough to shatter the walls of Jericho, but then began to flow from the stereo like golden syrup from a horn: Louis Armstrong. Dad and Mom had that record. A lot of older people owned it and listened as if it were something they had lost and never regained.

And we sat with our photographs.

October

The birches in the park outside our classroom windows started burning with October's intense colors. They stood out golden-yellow against the blood-red maples, exclamations against the gray skies. The classes squeaked on, like the chalk in the teacher's hand. He wrote and wrote on the board and we copied him. The air smelled of damp clothes and stuffiness. The next hour, screaming and dashing, we would rush into the gym and line up in front of old Rubberhead, our athletic instructor. He was always bouncing around, loved gymnastic exercises, especially the horizontal bar. To me, his class should be a breathing space, a spell of freedom in a gray day. Some could choose to go outdoors. Some might go to the pool, and those who felt they had to demonstrate their incredible vigor, could tie themselves up in knots if they wanted to. But no, it was either gymnastics or basketball. Pass, Idiot! Over here! Move it, Johnny!

The important point was to excel, to be first, to win, to compete bravely, to compare yourself with someone else and beat him with your own record, to run in a squirrel cage. Sometimes Rubberhead could be seen on a fine Sunday morning, puffing and springing along over stumps and stones. He was inexhaustible, young, enthusiastic—and slightly contemptuous of people like me.

I studied the faces around me. Some sat staring, and you never knew what they were staring at; perhaps they were dreaming inwardly, perhaps they built mental ships to escape in or watched how the teacher's Adam's apple bobbed up and down. Some carried on a whispered or not-so-whispered conversation, shot wads of paper, chewed gum and assumed solemn expressions when they sensed that they were being observed. And the teacher toiled and reached for whatever shreds of interest we might show, trying to hold our tiredness in check, trying to get us to listen. Hundreds of times, thousands of times, he had said the same things, written the same texts, stood before similarly pale, thin, autumnal faces that gradually turned dull and lifeless as paper, with the approach of Christmas.

Sometimes a new note could be heard, and the whole school suddenly livened up like a dynamo: shouts and yells when the first real snow swirled us around, drove us breathing heavily through the doors and up the stairs. At other times the note was lonely but constant, heard only by me. Once I shipped out aboard the *Beagle* and dove and glided along the dark, jutting edge of the cliff with silver bands of water bubbles purling behind me. I discovered fabulous new creatures, and geometric patterns suddenly became clear, obvious, and beautiful. I remember a geometry test during which I went on drawing; with a protractor and a sharp pen point I constructed the pattern of wave movements, endless curves, fan-shaped, singing lines: I'd forgotten the problem I was supposed to solve. And then the Goose—our mathematics teacher—showed my test to the class: "Johan has produced here an imaginative variant of an equilateral triangle which offers more evidence of his erratic artistic talents than of his interest in mathematics. I have no choice but to give a failing mark to this aesthetic masterpiece."

Failed. Examined. Approved. Passed with distinction. Admonished.

And the weariness of mornings growing darker every day. When the sun broke out from the clouds, we would turn our faces toward it; the classroom would fill with light, and crisscross patterns of the mullions would fall across the chill white walls. Sun reflected from the teacher's glasses. Perhaps he, too, wished to be somewhere else, off to some remote isle, to the Galapagos or Bow Island.

Now the trees around Söder's cottage would be standing like kindling wood. Paradise flamed bright before the gray and rain-laden ranks of November days. Not a soul on Bow Island. Water still as a mirror. Everyone back in their ant heaps. Dad and Mom at their jobs. Gerda sleeping after her much earlier morning shift, having already taken Marvin to his class for mentally retarded children. Marvin faced with the testing blocks. Nora at her class. Each of us in a class.

While autumn burned and burned.

Marvin's Room

Marvin sat on the edge of the bed in his kitchen alcove, with a picture book in his hands. It was a gray autumn day, warm and damp. Fog clung along the shore, hiding the rocks and the islands. On my way back from school I had stopped down by the docks and watched the slow, heaving swell of the water carrying broken planks, containers, litter. Not all the boats had been taken out of the water yet for the winter. Olle had asked if I'd go out with him around town after school. But I remembered that I had promised to visit Marvin, and said no. I would have liked to go. I sat on a chair facing Marvin in the kitchen. The silence was unbroken. Gerda was off cleaning in someone's house. She worked and slept in shifts.

"I don't know what it is," said Marvin. He sat rigidly upright, staring past me, away, past the kitchen table, the window, and out to the wall with its balconies across the yard.

"What's that?"

"There are more dead. Here there are more dead. They teach me all sorts of things, but here there are more dead. There's no ocean and there are no trees. There's one behind there."

He nodded toward the balconies.

"You mean the toothpick. That's a maple."

"We didn't have those home. It's like in a cage."

Marvin wiped his eyes with his shirtsleeve. He started rocking back and forth, and he breathed like a coffeepot about to boil over. He gave a whistling sound. His steam was up. The picture book fell from his hands, but he didn't notice it. I picked it up.

"Do you like it?"

"They're all wearing old clothes. They're dancing around a maypole."

"You could come with me to the library, and we could find something more fun for you."

Marvin stopped rocking.

"Or you could borrow some of my books."

"They have so many words."

He looked straight at me. "I don't know what it is."

He struck his face with his hand while he repeated, "I don't know what it is! I don't know it. All the leaves fall and the trees die. And they don't come back. They die. They go away and die. Gerda goes away, she won't come back again."

"Of course she'll come back," I said. "And I'll sit here until she does."

"It blows away and rains away."

"It's autumn. Then it'll be winter, and snow will fall and cover everything. The yard will be all white and clean. And then comes spring, and then all the trees will have buds and new leaves, because they don't die."

Marvin sat there with his face like a glossy white spot in the autumn twilight. I wanted to leave, go home to my room and my microscope, the transistor and the reading lamp; home to security. If only Gerda would come! Some heavy raindrops struck the windowpanes.

"Come on, let's go over to my place," I said.

I stood up and went into the living room: Gerda's bed with its crocheted bedspread, the round table and its four white chairs, the lampshade decorated with flowers.

"Have you a scrap of paper and a pen?" I asked.

Marvin went over to the bureau, opened a drawer, and took out letter paper and a pen. He sat down at the table. There was a vase with asters in it. He took the pen and hunched over the faintly lined paper. His hand remained motionless. It squeezed the pen so hard that his knuckles turned white.

"Wait, I'll help you."

I took his hand, but he pulled away from me.

"Now, don't be silly, of course you want to write a few lines to Gerda."

I took his hand again, and this time he let me do it. I wrote with his hand: I AM OVER AT JOHAN'S.

He spelled out the whole text. His hand had felt quite lifeless.

"She won't know who it is," he said. "She'll ask and won't know who."

He took the pen and drew a large *M*.

"Now she'll know," he said.

And he nodded, satisfied.

The air hit us in the entry, heavy and wet-smelling. The gutters spat out their overflow, but the rain was slackening off. We met Peter on the stairs. He stopped, his lips let out a sneer. "Look at the great buddies."

"Come," I urged Marvin.

Marvin walked straight ahead. Peter had to turn to one side. But Marvin was scared, I could see that. He almost ran up the stairs. We heard Peter's piercing whistle behind us.

"Don't bother about him," I said.

But Marvin stopped, grabbed the banister tightly. We turned. The stairwell was completely silent in the dim light; it smelled of linoleum. A door slammed.

Slowly Marvin sank down on a step.

I sat next to him and said, "We can look at my stamps. Want to? Or you can look in the microscope. Erik has a fantastic microscope."

Marvin was silent.

Suddenly a blast of music sounded from behind the Björklövs' door. Someone shouted something in a harsh, loud voice, then silence returned. We could see the shiny, wet asphalt in the yard and the darkness of Marvin's entry. We saw the toothpick, propped up with a stick, protected with chicken wire. It was more like a twig than a tree.

I didn't know what to say. Suddenly a thought passed through my mind, and I said quickly, "Remember the dolphins!"

Slowly Marvin let go of the banister. He wrinkled his dark eyebrows, his small eyes glowed. "When I'm scared, they come. But then I was dreaming. *Here* there aren't any."

"You'll see, there are some here. Come on!"

I took his arm and he got up willingly. We walked up the stairs and I unlocked our door. The familiar smell struck me, the smell of *home*, as distinct as if I'd struck a boulder. No one had come back yet. Marvin followed me into my room. He sat on my bed with his long arms dangling emptily. He looked around. "What do you have there?" he asked.

"Only a drawing pad and my crayons. Want them?"

I put the pad in his lap and gave him the crayons. I said, "Today I dreamed I was a sea lion gliding through the ocean as light as a feather. It was like dancing. The water was turquoise-green. I could breathe. I didn't have to struggle up to the surface. And it was light very deep down there."

Marvin nodded. His hand drew dark-blue depths, and an orange sun which almost burned a hole in the pad. He drew easily, without hesitation. But he chose the colors scrupulously, examining each crayon. On a clifftop, he drew a deer. Its antlers were red and stuck up into the sky. He became involved in drawing, and I didn't have to stay with him. I got out my biology notebook, sat down at my desk, and went through the week's lessons. It was quiet and peaceful; we didn't have to say anything to each other. When I lit the bedside lamp, Marvin didn't react, he went right on drawing. He drew dolphins in the ocean, dark shadows in a blue ocean. There they were. He enticed them, entrapped them. He drew his most beautiful dreams.

Matti and Gerda

Gerda had bought a nameplate for the door; it read: *Lundgren*. I rang, and a strange man opened the door. He said, right off,

"You're Johan?"

"Yes."

"Come in."

He had a dark, sharply angular face and thin hair combed straight back. There was something birdlike about him. But his hands were large and broad, his shoulders powerful. He said,

"My name is Matti. I'm a driver at the factory where Gerda cleans. Gerda is in town with Marvin. They'll be back in a little while. Have a seat."

He studied me closely. I felt disappointed. He must have had a key to the apartment.

"I understand that you're Marvin's best friend."

"I like Marvin a lot. He's good."

"Good? He's difficult, what with his illness and all. You have to be careful with him, but not too careful."

He lit a cigarette, thoughtfully.

"What do you mean?"

"I mean you have to give him orders sometimes, otherwise nothing happens. He needs proper attention. A lot of people pamper their children, and with Marvin, that's all too easy."

"Gerda has certainly never done that."

"Maybe not."

"But they're not happy here."

"They don't have any choice. Besides, it's going better and better. Gerda is very capable and reliable. My family comes from the islands, too. I remember how it was—tough. I quit studying after grade school and got a job. Whenever there was a chance I got out on the water. Borrowed a rowboat or stole one. Sometimes there's no choice, is there?"

I didn't say anything.

"We're both city kids now, aren't we? Anyway, you look as if you came right up out of the asphalt. Or like a potato in a cellar."

He grinned at me; he had even, white teeth and a dark stubble on his chin. I didn't know whether I liked him or not. Something about him frightened me.

He killed the cigarette, half-smoked, in the lid of a coffee can. He said,

"Naturally you read a lot?"

"Yes."

He made a face. "Fancy language, foreign words. No, I've no time for all that. Or interest, either, to be polite. People who read—do they get any smarter? You can take it all in from TV."

" 'Take it all in?' "

"That's right, Mr. Private Philosopher."

"Then you're just stuck with what they chew over for you."

"Your dad told you that."

"So what?"

"Okay. Go on."

"I think that you can't do anything yourself with TV, you can't be imaginative, or change anything, or add or take anything away. The pictures are just there. With a book it's different. Take . . . take Marvin. He talks about dolphins who'll help him if he's drowning."

"Dolphins? I haven't heard that one. But he sure rattles on when he gets going. There aren't any dolphins this far north, are there?"

"In books you can read about things that don't exist. On TV, people can only learn about the way things are."

"Watch out you don't go off the deep end with all your dreams. You've got to have your feet on the ground, or everything goes to hell."

"And Marvin?"

"What about Marvin?"

"He needs his dreams. For him they're important, more important than for the rest of us. They help him."

"Maybe so."

"Besides, don't you ever dream?"

"Sure, we all dream sometimes, at night. That's different."

"No, it's not."

There was a noise at the door; Gerda and Marvin came in. Marvin walked right over and sat down. He leaned forward, with the brim of his cap pulled down over his eyes.

"You should see. Every window is lit up. Some have dolls, and there was a car in one window. You bump into people everywhere. They bump into me all the time. There were pigeons on the road. They were dirty and lazy and sat there in front of the cans, but they weren't run over. And there was a stairs you couldn't walk on, it rolled up. Everything makes a racket, too, and everyone is in a hurry. The grass has fences around it."

"Dear Marvin, you've already seen all that before," said Gerda, sitting down heavily. "We'll never be real city people. How my feet ache! And I forgot to start dinner."

"I'll fix it," said Matti. "Sit still. I've been having an uplifting conversation with the professor here."

He disappeared with a few quick dance steps.

Gerda looked tired.

"How's the cleaning going?"

"It's heavy work. I'm still not used to it. It's one thing to scrub your own floor on your own time. This is a shift job and the early morning hours are the worst. How people use paper! It's insane. Paper everywhere. The scrap baskets are always full. And the carpets I have to sweep. They call it office landscaping, with flowers and music. Then you should see our canteen. Only room for three of us at a time."

Her red, chapped hands rested in front of her. She was wearing her hair drawn back; she looked pretty. She added,

"But we're alive. And Marvin is going to his course,

and Matti has promised to get him a job in a warehouse. A sorting job."

"I walked down the streets," said Marvin. "I know them all. I've learned them." 1904730

He hauled out a well-thumbed map of the city. "Just ask me."

"Which streets do you take from here to the Square?"

"Sea Street. The Strand. Turn to the right. Sailors Lane. Skippers Street. Go across University Square. Then straight down Harbor Street."

"You know a lot!"

"A sorting job means you stand or sit all day long in a room, Marvin."

"Matti will fix it for me. I'll walk right. I'll show Gerda the way home. Matti has taught me."

I felt a prick of envy. Matti came in with glasses and plates. When he had finished setting the table, he looked at Gerda:

"After dinner you're going to lie down."

"Do I look that tired?"

Marvin looked at Gerda and then at Matti, and before Matti could answer her, he blurted out,

"I know all the streets, I see everything. There are streets with trees, and thin streets where only thin people grow. Like you."

He pointed at Matti.

Matti laughed. "I'm not all that thin, Marvin. We're really more or less the same, when it comes right down to it."

"There are different streets and different people. Those who want to, and those who don't."

"Want to what?" asked Matti.

"Help," I said. "Those who want to, and those who don't. Pushy people, and those who aren't pushy. Some who run, and others who stop and listen. Right, Marvin?"

He nodded, rocked his body, and nodded. His face shone in the cone of bright light cast by the lamp shade, then sank back into the room's warm, mellow darkness.

Friday

Mild, gray autumn days, when the trees still haven't lost their leaves but turn to flame, golden, orange, blood-red in the rain-glistening parks; when the city seems a mellow space where people live alone and yet not alone. Even school, the teachers, and schoolmates don't seem as tough on days like these: you wait for them. You calmly collect your things when the bell rings, you don't hurry down the stairs. It's Friday, best of all days. You walk slowly out into the schoolyard and beyond onto the street. Shop windows glow brightly. Hundreds of things caught in a single glance: colorful record covers, endless rows of sticky pastries in bakery windows, posters outside movie houses, neon signs blinking on and off, the smell of gas, the patchwork of book jackets in the bookstore, candies from all over the world, bright fruits!

And you don't want any of it—except maybe a movie camera that you know is too expensive—but still . . . you don't want anything, you look at it all with curiosity, rather indifferently; you stroll along the esplanade, perhaps with some school chums, sit in a café, count makes of cars. Light flashes from windows, the cool taste of a glass on the tongue; you let the minutes go by. School is forgotten in flashes of life and traffic around you. Mild, gray autumn days when you can plan your evening. You come home to everything so familiar: the smell of cooking, the lingering smell of a soldering iron in your room, the reading lamp with its green shade, soft pop music on the radio. Rain begins to patter on the roof outside, out in the dark.

A light shines in the entry; perhaps Marvin is reading or looking at pictures in one of the *National Geographics* I lent him. He looks at iguanas and rice fields, bright blossoms, palm trees, or icebergs with thousands of penguins. The rain falls, relentlessly. Is he remembering autumns on Bow Island, the storms, the eternal thundering of the ocean, the loneliness and dampness? Foggy days when the water lies smooth and black, when the reeds, brittle yet strong, rustle gently down along the wet shoreline; high tide, the jetty almost under water, darkness and the oil lamp in the room where no one is living now, the empty room where the wind may be howling through a broken window. Across on the mainland sit Söder and Nora, while the fishnet casts its fine mesh pattern on the ceiling and the parrot utters his complaining "Rrrroaaaa rrroaaaa!" The radio over in Nora's corner is playing the same music that I hear in my room, and she, like me, looks out the window: rain. The barometer on the captain's bridge falls and falls, and

Söder follows all the daily news with his finger—murders, war, political speeches—while the wind rises, there, in Paradise.

I looked around my room as if it were both very familiar and yet foreign, unknown. There was a piece of paper in front of me. My hand slowly wrote: *Johan Bergman, 26 Sea Street, Helsingfors, Finland, Scandinavia, Europe, The World, The Universe.* Then my hand slowly crossed out everything except my name and *Sea Street.* That seemed enough. You couldn't see the universe. There was nothing but mild, damp, low clouds when night fell, and the mirror image of a white desk, a green lamp, a thin, indistinct face slowly coming into focus: Johan Bergman, fourteen years old, student. This evening I'd go to the library. Two free days stretched out before me, I could do anything I wanted with them, no one could destroy them; they were mine.

I felt happy without needing to explain why. I knew that people were dying, suffering, getting shot, starving to death. If I didn't have some of this free, happy feeling inside me, how could I ever help them? I thought of Marvin—his face lighting up from deep within his eyes as if you put on a light in there; Marvin, who was "ill," "backward," had "brain damage"; the children shouted "Idiot!" at him sometimes, when they felt safe in a group, and they threw stones at him. But he must feel joy, too. It was like a warm light that went hand in hand with autumn and dusk, with the darkness outside, light and dark following each other like waves.

I could hear wailing and yelling down in the courtyard. Dad Berglund was back home after ten beers,
giving Peter a beating. He stopped and pounded on
one of the garbage cans: Damn! Damn! Damn! And
then he was dragged off home as usual by Mrs. Berglund, a woman who could move mountains. They disappeared up the stairs of C entry. Where did Peter go
off to? Then I thought about nights when I lay in
bed waiting for Mom and Dad to come home from
some party. I'd hear Dad's loud voice on the stairs,
turn off my light, and pretend to be asleep. Maybe
Peter sat down to dinner and let the storm rage and
studied his father's face, indifferently as usual, that
broad face, dark as an oven door and equally expres-
sionless. People were everywhere, but there was only
one Johan Bergman. No one else like him anywhere
on earth, sitting at a white desk, writing his name
while the rain fell like a sleepy, monotonous song on
all the city roofs. I opened the book on my desk.

"Are we off again?"

"No, on the contrary, we're losing altitude!"

"Worse than that, Mr. Cyrus! We're crashing!"

"Good God! Throw out the ballast!"

"Here goes the last sack!"

I knew it almost by heart, the exclamations, the
words. They were like echoes in the silence. I lay my
head down on the book and closed my eyes. But it felt
as if they were still open and I was looking out into
other rooms, where strangers sat talking words that I
didn't hear and yet understood. I didn't know whether
I was awake or dreaming. I might be dreaming that I
wasn't dreaming, with Cyrus Smith, Spillett, Nab, Pen-

croff, and Harbert, swaying, sinking, swaying, sinking, until I slept and awoke at last when Mom stroked my hair and whispered in my ear, "Dinner's ready." Or maybe I dreamed that, too.

Colt Island

One glorious day with a springlike blue sky and the
sun shining on each dying leaf, we made an excursion
to Colt Island with Gerda and Marvin. The bright
sky and the sun made me feel restless and out of
place with the autumn and one of those Sundays so end-
lessly long that it has to be filled with excursions and
activity so that we can handle it. We strolled about in
a mild wind and found our way to the center of town.
The city was windy and deserted; not many people
lived in the center any more, they drove in from
their suburbs to go to the movies and drove home
again afterward. Beautiful old houses had disappeared;
glass skyscrapers replaced them. On workdays they
beamed with fluorescent brightness, but on Sundays
they were dark and empty. The grass was still August-
green under all the leaves, and something like a violet
head of cabbage was growing on the esplanade.

Gerda and Mom walked ahead and we followed.
Now and then Marvin stopped, as if to check on the
wind or see that the clouds were moving in the right

direction, that nature was following its laws. He was observant. He noticed how the crows flew out of skylights in the old, well-to-do houses, how the row of flags hung slack on the bank's bragging facade. He noticed the old men sitting drinking in the park. He marveled over a miniature poodle with tufts and ruffs in poodle fashion followed by its mistress with tufts and ruffs in lady fashion. In the bus, he stared out the window and kept twisting his head around. When the bus drove by an inlet, with an autumn look to it, he got up and pointed,

"There! Look!"

There it was. The ocean. Far away, you could see a fine plume of smoke. Closer by, heavy, dark clouds rose from five smokestacks of factories that worked day and night. The distillery had expanded: liquor for everyone. The greediest customers settled down on their park benches and stiffened along with the autumn. Marvin stood up in the bus, and I felt my ears burning red. People stared. Tree trunks and glittering water sped past us.

Marvin turned to me. "He'll drive all the way there!"

"Sure he will. Sit down so you don't disturb him."

"Will he drive to Bow Island? All the way there?"

Light shifted on Marvin's face as the sun streamed in and out and clouds drifted past the windows.

Gerda turned and rested her hand on Marvin's. She said, "We're having an outing, Marvin. Calm yourself and sit down. That way you can see better."

Marvin sat down, looked out the window. His hands fidgeted restlessly. He couldn't express everything he was thinking. He couldn't put it into words. Sometimes they came out halfway or askew, tumbled from his mouth against his will, stopped in his throat or in his head. There was so much to see. So much that no one else saw. Sometimes I could almost feel how he was thinking, just for a second. It felt very strange, as if I were a spy or someone else, a stranger, his *real* friend.

The bus pulled over and stopped. It emptied quickly. Marvin remained seated.

"Come on, Marvin!" I took him by the arm.

"Next time I'm going further. Because this is a good bus, it has a Volvo motor. But it was built here, in Finland. I read that."

We strolled out on the wooden bridge and looked at the city and the stadium tower, the pale, autumnal water and the quacking wild ducks. Marvin tossed bits of bread to them from a bag that Mom had brought along. They quarreled and jabbed at each other viciously. Some were always left out and never got anything.

"They should take turns," said Marvin.

A light breeze stirred the water to an almost summery liveliness, but along the shore big maple leaves like the palms of hands floated by, and when the sun passed behind a cloud, there was a real nip in the air.

Gerda said to Mom, "If you've been looking after yourself all your life, you feel it in your back when you get down on your knees all day for other people. That's the most difficult thing, and also the fact that you're watched. So it's a real break to get out on a day like this. Matti has promised to drive us over to Söder's someday before Christmas. He's arranged a job for Marvin now."

"How do you think that will work out?"

"It has to. It's so important. Marvin is very excited about it. He's like a very diligent child, so it ought to suit him. I've talked with the foreman. Marvin can start on a trial basis next month."

Gulls flew by, crying harshly now and then. The huge firs stretched their dark branches; if you leaned your head back, you could scarcely see all the way to the top because of their circling branches. Marvin put himself in the shade of an old cowshed and stroked the silvery old logs. "Yes. It's alive. It really is."

"What does it say?" I asked.

"The shed? Ha, it can't talk," answered Marvin, grinning. "You know that. It can't say anything."

A squirrel scampered along the path, stood up on its back legs, studied us with its bright button eyes, clasped its hands, and said grace briefly.

"Here, take this," said Mom, offering Marvin a bag of nuts.

Marvin took a fistful and filled his mouth, chewing eagerly.

"No, they're for the squirrel," I explained.

I put some nuts in his hand. He sat still. The squirrel hopped nearer, grabbed a nut quickly, jumped a step backward, sat munching it hastily. Then it disappeared among the rustling leaves.

"I could have caught him," said Marvin. "Had him in my hand and held him fast."

"Then he would really have been scared."

Marvin wrinkled his forehead. "Y-e-e-s."

He looked away into the distance and then suddenly said, in a small voice, "I want to go home."

"Come see an interesting boat and don't worry so much. Look what a beautiful autumn day it is."

We wandered into the dark boathouse. It smelled of tar and the islands. Inside was an old boat from the islands that people used to use to row to Sunday services; long and narrowly built, like a big peapod.

"They were already a thing of the past when I was a little girl," said Gerda. "But Dad used to tell about the boat races every Midsummer Day."

"Look, Marvin, this is a church boat, people used to row it to church on Sundays," Dad explained.

"It's Sunday today," said Marvin. "But it won't go out. It's lying here empty."

Hoarse gull cries flocked in through gaps in the log walls. We made our way out, strolled up the path to the old wooden church. Mom laid her arm around my shoulder. Suddenly Gerda stopped.

"Where's Marvin?"

"He must still be in the boathouse," Dad answered. He turned quickly and started almost running. I ran after him and we plunged into the darkness and the smell of tar: total silence there.

My voice sounded like a hoarse whistle when I called out, "Marvin!"

Only the wind whined through the walls. By now, Gerda and Mom had come.

"He isn't here. He must have gone another way."

"No," said Gerda. "He's frightened. He wouldn't go out into the open on his own. Not Marvin. Marvin!"

she shouted, but not sternly, just gently and firmly. "Marvin? I'm here."

There was a rustling sound from a dark bundle in the prow of the boat. I leaned over the gunwale. He had crouched down like a bundle, his face was very white and all crumpled.

"He's here," I called slowly. "Come help!"

We got him up, helped him out of the boat, supported him. He said nothing, just whimpered now and then. We started walking back toward the city. By the bridge with the ducks, he had already started walking more independently; in the bus back, he was calm but silent. We separated in the courtyard, each going to our own apartment.

"Whenever he starts thinking about Bow Island, he has a hard time," said Mom. "He doesn't forget. It's as if it is a shock to him every time."

We were sitting at the kitchen table in our overcoats, talking about Marvin.

"What will happen now?" I wondered. "When he starts the sorting job?"

I pictured Marvin under a pale 100-watt bulb hanging from a thin cord. Cartons, bales, packages, paper. Cold fluorescent tubes, no windows. He would move about there like a bird in a cage. He would lie down sometimes, all huddled up, when the world became too much for him, the way we all curl up sometimes in our beds to protect ourselves from everything pressing in upon us. He saw and felt things so much quicker than we did. We had taught ourselves: You don't do that.

I sensed that he was afraid, but I couldn't understand him all the time. He was a stranger, even when he was so close to me.

"What will happen?" I wondered again.

And Mom answered like Gerda, "It has to work out. It's important for him. He knows that himself."

"And what if it doesn't? What if he fails?"

We were silent.

Finally Dad said, "Then we'll have to help them. Because even Marvin has to learn how to survive failure. Who knows, maybe he'll grow, mature, if he can make it. . . ."

It was getting darker. People were turning on lights in their rooms, each in his own room. And wind rattled the windows.

Nora in the City

I heard the mail slot rattle open and something heavy
fall on the doormat. I listened. I heard an owl's "Hoo
hooo hooo!" from somewhere in the echoing stairwell.
I jumped up and rushed out through the kitchen.
A red stone lay there on the mat, like a piece of the
ocean floor, worn smooth by waves. Like sand at the
water's edge on clear summer mornings. I pulled open
the door. The stairs always shone so clean and smelled
of pine soap. Hooo! Hooo! I ran out and leaned over
the banister. Peering up at me was an owl face with
two huge, round, black-framed eyes. Nora!

"Nora! Come on up!"

Mrs. Ewert across from us opened her door, stood
there thin as a lily and sharp as a compass point, her
face like a triangle: "What in all creation!"

"This creation is an owl from Paradise out here in
the cold!" curtsied Nora, clattering up the stairs. Then
she studied Mrs. Ewert carefully and Mrs. Ewert's
embroidered housecoat, as if she were an interesting

insect. Then, turning to me, Nora went on, "Is she kind? She looks it, deep inside."

Mrs. Ewert stood there as if turned to stone, then slammed her door with a tremendous, unprecedented bang. Something seemed to jangle and crash all at once in Mrs. Ewert's geometric life.

"Have you many like that in this entry?" Nora asked.

"Nothing wrong with her but her nerves," I said, sounding like my mother. "After all, we don't have owls appear on our stairs every day! Nora! How great to see you! Come in! Tell me everything!"

And while she shoved me down our hall, I went on asking, "Why are you in town? How's Söder? Have you seen Marvin? How did you get time off from school?"

Tears almost came to my eyes from eagerness.

Nora sat down on one of the white wooden chairs with high, turned-wood backs that we had around our kitchen table. She raised her index finger and checked off the fingers of her other hand at right angles to it.

"I'm in town to talk with the doctor about Dad. Söder has palpitations and is only just making it, he says. I met Marvin in the warehouse. I got permission because of this special situation. And now I'm here to see how you are."

She looked around.

"Do you still have the skiff?"

"She's been tarred. She's waiting for you."

Outside, it was peaceful and light; snow was falling like a white curtain, calmly and gently. Nora's dark hair was still wet. She was wearing it pulled back, like Gerda. She got up, walked into my room, and looked around: "This isn't too bad. For a boy's room, I mean."

"How's that?"

"It's nicely painted and not too untidy. Obviously, your mom cleans up. Have you had a lot of hassle since I saw you last?"

"Not exactly."

"You're evading. That's good. There are plenty of people with elbows, Söder says, and too few hands. Like these here."

She stretched out her hands, thin, strong, still suntanned. I took them, held them. Nora looked at me with her clear, dark eyes, and said,

"Marvin's holding on as if it's a question of life or death, as if he's drowning. Is he?"

I looked at her. She saw my hesitation about answering. She nodded slowly, a shadow crossed her face. She let go of my hands, her gaze suddenly very distant. It was very silent and simple in my room, as though both of us could talk or do without talking; nothing was forcing us. Maybe the November snow did this; maybe the glance from behind a pair of big round glasses, or a head lowering.

Then Nora slapped her forehead, shook herself, saying,

"I drifted off just then. You have to, it's important sometimes. You can't always just stay right here on the ground. Not when it's a question of Marvin. Remember what I taught you."

"That stories are important," I answered.

"And to be silent."

"And to have secrets."

"And to be able to wait. Watch and wait. Marvin—"
She broke off, silent awhile.

"He's not happy here, neither is Gerda," I said.

"We have to wait. They're hoping for so much.
Marvin said that he didn't know what the trees do
when they die. Or whether they'll live. And that you
told him they would. Though who'd believe it, looking at the trees in your backyard, they all look
blighted and tortured."

"Not all of them. Not in the big parks. We have
huge, ancient trees there—red maples, larches, enormous conifers. Some of them are protected by law."

"Lucky for them. But some park trees have been so
clipped that they look like tails."

She added thoughtfully, "And then Marvin said that
he wasn't dreaming. He really wants to be a bird."

"Did he talk about the dolphins?"

She nodded, "His guardian angels, whenever he
talks about dying."

Suddenly she clasped her hands together and burst
out, "If only Söder had some. Just one."

She rested her head in her hands, and I said, "He
has! Maybe we all have!"

"Phooey!"

Nora sniffed, rubbed her eyes, and added, "Marvin's job is to sort paper in different piles. He has to
move paper from the right to the left and paper from
the left to the right. Then he stamps them. Bam!
Bam! They put a supervisor on him, too, and he's
managing. When he caught sight of me, he nearly lost
the whole idea of what he was supposed to be doing.
The words gushed out, you know how it can be with

Marvin. The place smelled of glue and dust. Then suddenly he stopped talking, as if someone were watching him. He simply got scared, scared of himself. He started moving papers again. He was so caught up in his work that he didn't hear me leave. That was good, in a way. That makes it easier."

"Perhaps they'll manage."

"Perhaps."

And she added, "Gerda has a punch card and a clock. So they can measure out her life in seconds."

"Good God," she said later. "Poor human beings."

"Are you hungry?" I asked.

"Of course. I've brought some homebaked bread we can dunk. Let's make coffee. Incidentally, where are the old folks?"

"Dad and Mom? At work. They'll be home around five."

"Then we can talk in peace and quiet. Things get so messed up when adults are around."

As I followed her into the kitchen, she said over her shoulder, "The bull on the big farm is impotent."

"What?"

"True. He doesn't mount any more, he's no good. He just stands there glaring, ashamed of himself. He can't get it up any more. It happens, as Söder used to say, in the best families. Then once he got nasty and crashed through the gate and dashed head-on at the food truck and Emil had to slam on the brakes. But he just turned and stopped and shitted on everything and then trotted in through the church gates just when there was a wedding going on. Jesus, that was a speedy wedding march."

"You mean he went into the church?"

"No, he wasn't quite that religious. But he did go into the churchyard. What a commotion."

She settled her chin in her hands and looked out through the window at the winter. "Everything needs that."

"What?"

"A little more of a stir in the churchyard. A little more cheer. A little more life, more light, not only on Christmas Eve. Everything there is white now. The same with all of Paradise."

"Has the ice set in yet?"

"Some, around the reeds, but it'll be firm by January."

Dusk was falling. The water boiled, Nora poured it. I felt as if we'd always sat there so cozily. Nora studied me.

"You look pale. Have you been ill?"

I shook my head.

"Do you have any friends?"

"A few."

"Have the Lundgrens?"

"Gerda has a—friend. A driver from the factory."

"Hmmm."

Nora pointed at the geranium in the kitchen window. "I wrote a song about that!"

"Sing it!"

"Here goes."

Then Nora sang in her sturdy, piercing voice, "The geranium, our love's reddest rose! Can never wither, its scent never goes."

She repeated the lines to make sure. Then she said,

"You always hear that kind of thing on the radio."

"Have you got a TV?"

"We got ourselves a little one, but we seldom turn it on. Söder says that most of the people you see on it are fabricated. They all have opinions and they want us all to think the same way. But the motorboat accident we saw, that was fine. Two policemen drowned, because the government had given them such a rotten, miserable boat. That was in Hitis. It wasn't political, it was about people. And then we saw birds in South America, and a boy who was rather like Marvin. But usually we prefer to read."

"Me, too!"

"Good!" said Nora. "Mrs. Lundvall started vomiting and the baby came in the boat on the way to the hospital, so they had to cut the umbilical cord and do everything right there out on the water. But it wasn't blowing too hard, so it all went well. They landed at our place because it was the shortest route. The baby was all red and wrinkled. They lay on our sofa bed until the ambulance came."

"Tell me more!"

"I'm not telling stories!"

"Well, almost. I mean, so little happens here!"

"Little! Here in the city? Things happen here all the time. You just have to listen and watch carefully. There's a doctor in our school, he darts in suddenly during our classes, pokes his head in just like this, peers around, says, 'Go on!' and then his head disappears, as if someone had pulled a string. Like this."

I sat listening. It was like being transported to Nora's corner in the cottage, her white, cane-bottomed chair, the desk, the books, the bunk bed with its embroidered cushions, the windowpanes and their view out over the pines and the sea. Yes, it was as if I heard the muted murmur of the sea, near and far, the city's ocean and the ocean of the islands, which were one and the same, slowly talking, falling silent, talking again. And I thought how Nora was the kind of person who creates a space around her where you can feel at home. And how people like that are really essential to our survival, because so many people build no space at all, or else they only destroy spaces, and rooms, one after another, tear down and tear down more and more. When I looked at her, I thought about how she could never be changed, how she'd always sit opposite me at a table telling me things, fables and true stories, more fantastic for being true. Yet they were believable, whether happy or sorrowful, because they were right and real, just as everything honest and straight in Nora is real.

"Hello! Wake up! You can't steer a barge and have a conversation if you're off in the fog! Carl, you know, Söder's cousin, he once invented a machine to get rid of the fog. You cranked it, it had two wings, he built it out of an old bicycle. He drove it out into the fog and cranked it, out on the ice. We shouted and shouted, trying to find him. He didn't want to answer, just sat there cranking away. He got frostbite in his toes, and the fog machine blew away in the wind. He was called 'Cranking Carl' after that, and he didn't like it. He never married."

Nora glanced at the clock. "Heavens! I have to be

at the doctor's at five! So long. God bless you. I'm going to be late."

And at the door she shouted, "I'll call or come!"

Then she was gone, only the echo of an owl remained in the stairwell. The kitchen was empty; for a while it had been Nora's room.

The Library

Out of the darkness from the ocean, snow whirled against us, carried by the wind through the swaying cones of light cast by the streetlamps. Wind whistled in the treetops. They grasped at the low sky ineffectually, with an old man's fingers. White drifts accumulated in the lee of street corners. Marvin wore his winter cap pulled down. Snow stuck to his long dark coat, he trudged on, leaning into the wind. He shouted,

"Dad drowned in a snowstorm like this!"

"Is that really true?"

"His motor broke down. He sank."

We rounded the corner into the square. All the way down the row of old houses, only a single window was lit. The powerful winter whirled over the dark, slippery paving stones, and the eagle on the statue of the Czarina was ready to take off into the darkness, one really strong blast of wind could rip it from its perch. A foghorn blared out somewhere along the horizon

of the ocean. Marvin stopped, grabbed and hugged
my arm.

"Now he's barking!"

"That's a ship heading for the harbor!" I shouted.
"She'll sink!"

"No! She's just signaling that she's going to dock!"

I dragged him along. It was as if the snowstorm
had given me wings; I loved it. My skin, body, and
eyes loved it: the swirling snow, the exertion, the
wildly swaying streetlamps, one solitary lit window;
something to battle against, something to strive for.
Really frigid weather hadn't set in yet, there was mild-
ness in the strong wind, bringing smells of the ocean
into the city, so that you could feel your skin alive
and glowing and could breathe easily. The cathedral's
clock face shone like a pale moon among driving
clouds of snow. No, it wasn't dark, but light! When
winter comes, the streets and yards are lit up, and on
overcast days, clouds capture light from the city.
Everything ugly is hidden beneath clean white snow.
People breathe clean air, streets become paths in the
snow. Children run about and make snowballs in
the park; every voice and sound is muted, clear,
distanced. The thinnest branches of the trees stand
out distinctly, and lights in the parks cast pale-violet
circles over undisturbed snowdrifts. When the storm
is over, the city, smiling, steps out onto its stairs and
into its squares, wrapped in expectation.

We struggled down the esplanade and made our
way to the library. It smelled of damp clothes. The
stairs were all wet, but inside it was quiet; most peo-

ple stayed home on evenings like this. Marvin checked with me,

"Have you got the card?"

"Yes, of course! It's in one of the books."

"Then you have the books?"

"Right here!"

"Then I can have more about ships. Old ships."

Marvin returned the books himself. He was solemn, as if something important were taking place. Maybe it was. All the soil and sustenance of dreams and curiosity was there. We clattered up to the third floor, found our way to the familiar shelf of the history of boats. Had any new books come in?

We looked, leafed through some. Wind battered the windows between the bookcases. Books everywhere, full of words, pictures, all read, written—how strange! The girl passing by with a book trolley stopped: "Can I help you?"

"We're looking for books about old sailing ships," I explained.

"My dad sailed in an old ship. It was covered with sails," said Marvin. He became excited, saliva dribbled from the corners of his mouth.

"Have you looked on the folio shelf?"

"What's that?"

"Where the big books are kept. Look, over here."

There they were. The big picture books. Ships in storms, color plates, Chapman's fleet of the skerries, old brigs, the Aland ferry boats, all the different kinds of boats. Marvin felt like going over to the information desk, where he said thanks and shook hands. The lady looked startled. She smiled.

"Dad sailed. Then he came home. Then later he drowned."

"Was he a sailor?"

"Then the dolphins came and carried him away."

The lady looked at him, "And where did they carry him?"

"To heaven."

"Yes, of course. How stupid I am. Would you like a book about dolphins?"

"Is there one?"

"There are always a few. If they are in."

We followed her up even more stairs. Narrow as stairs to a steeple, to the books about plants and animals. Marvin sat on a ladder for the shelves. He held the books as if they were a child on his lap. His eyes followed every move the librarian made.

"Here's one. But there's rather a lot of text and not many pictures."

"Gerda can read it to me, and I'll learn."

His face was glowing.

Marvin moved among the bookcases as if he had always been around there. It was as if he had changed, grown happier, more outgoing, as if he could look after himself better, as if he were not afraid. There was so much to touch, to leaf through, to spell out. The book bag became swollen with books. We stood in line at the loan desk. Marvin put the books down and said,

"Will I be in the picture?"

The woman took them, smiling, "Maybe! Sometime. Now we just make a record of the file card."

When we were out on the street again in the fresh air, we noticed that the wind had dropped. The scraping of snow clearing mingled with the softly muted sounds of cars rolling past. Marvin picked up some snow in his mitten and pressed it against his cheek. Then he said,

"I'm going to read by myself. I'll take each word separately, you understand, and read it, and then later I'll put them all together. Right? Then I'll say them. Won't that be good?"

"Just fine."

Occasionally a gust blew some snow down into our faces, off one of the black-and-white-flecked roofs. Marvin pointed to a sign: MEDAX.

"Like that dog he had when he came to hunt. A thin little one, this high off the ground."

"A dachshund."

"Yes. A dachshund. But what are the *M* and the *E* doing there?"

"That's a company."

"A company dachshund. That dog barked all the time. It wanted to bite the birds. I was angry with it. I was angry with him, too. You shouldn't shoot."

Out toward the ocean, the sky turned dark, lonesome.

Marvin walked faster, and I had a hard time keeping up with him.

"Marvin, don't walk so fast!"

He didn't hear me. The book bag was slung over his shoulder, his hands were plunged deep in his pockets, and the earflaps of his winter cap flapped like a big dog's ears. I almost ran after him. Suddenly he stopped, grabbed my upturned collar. He was quite upset.

"Is it true that the trees don't die? How can they live without leaves? They'll turn to ice, because they don't have any blood! They'll get knocked down! People chop and saw them down. Like Peter. He always wants to hit."

"Listen, Marvin. I've told you hundreds of times, and I'll say it again: They don't die. They're not dying. Every spring they get green and living again. Why did you think of that right now?"

Marvin was silent.

"And don't worry about Peter. He only wants to get attention. And if you don't let him bother you, he calms down."

"There, in the park, there was a big pile of branches. Didn't you see it? They've broken their arms. Their arms lay there bleeding, but no one saw it. Didn't you see it?"

"Sure I did, Marvin. But those were just dead branches that people were clearing away."

"There, you see! They do die!"

"Marvin. Remember how you had to clean up your garden? So it could grow. It's the same with trees here in the city. They have to be cleaned up and tidied so that they can grow and get big and leafy. Come, we have to go home. Think of all the books we have. About ships and dolphins."

Marvin stared out toward the harbor and the darkness. His face was all wet with snow. An ambulance with its siren wailing sped through the city, moving off into the distance. When we neared Sea Street, light shone in all the windows. People moved about there throughout the long winter, sitting and reading, looking at TV, getting up in the morning, going to work, coming home, eating, talking, sleeping. In the courtyard protected from the wind, it was calm and still; a few snowflakes slowly whirled their way down. I felt that I had returned from a long, long journey. That was often the way it was to be with and talk with Marvin. I looked up into his mute, intense face.

"Come on. Gerda's waiting."

Silently we walked into the dark, wet entry.

Fever

I waded slowly on through the burning sand, under the white sun. Somewhere nearby I saw Dad and Mom gradually sinking. And I was sinking, too. Far off, a man riding a horse could be seen. He galloped toward us, hooves tossing up sand. The sky dazzled our eyes sharply. I tried to shout, but I'd already sunk down too deep. My mouth filled with sand. With totally clear vision I watched myself sinking. I made a last, desperate effort, heaved myself up, and focused my wide, staring eyes into my silent bedroom. I was drenched with sweat.

I slowly drifted back into the same dream. Now the sand spread like snow over wide expanses. I looked right up into the darkening universe, cornflower blue, blue-black. Somewhere up there was a star, I knew that. Somewhere nearby, deliverance. I lay as in an ocean, slowly rocking. From up above, a star approached, a clear, shining orb. It rushed through the wintry streets, nearer, nearer. I couldn't escape, couldn't avoid crashing into whatever was rushing toward me but which at the same time remained elusive; or was I the one rushing on through space? And just before that unknown collided with me, I woke again.

I heard the door open, and Mom came in. "What is it? A nightmare?"

"Did I scream?"

"Yes, and you feel feverish."

"I mustn't get ill before Christmas. I mustn't."

"You can't help it. Go to sleep now."

I didn't hear when they left. When I awoke again, it was after twelve. Winter peered in mildly through my window under the half-drawn shades. I felt safe, unreal. I lay half-dreaming with the covers tucked up under my chin, delighting in this unexpected freedom, this extra day of my life when everything stayed at a distance and I moved across fields while still lying in my bed, the center of my universe. We're rising! We're falling! Throw everything overboard!

I drank some cold tea and nibbled on a sour-rye biscuit that tasted of warm summers. It was refreshing, like being in the hammock under the trees, where the shadows of the trees move to and fro over the ground. Marvin walked toward me, he gazed at me very intently but said nothing, his face paled away into blankness. How nice to let all your limbs rest, feel their own weight, nice not to make any effort, not to struggle, just be carried away.

Toward evening I sat up and read. I had four pillows behind me, three more books on the night table, a glass of juice, crackers, pen and paper. I couldn't wish for anything more. The city could run and walk

and spin in circles without me. The TV could blink
its blind eye without me. I was alone, with everything.
My bed was a flying carpet, and what I read took me
wherever I wished: out into dreams, into the world
around me. I lay protected in my warmth, while outside the wind pounded on the metal roofs with its
powerless giant fists.

The Christmas Trip

Eskil came to meet us at the bus stop in his Range Rover. He had frost on his beard and looked appropriately like Santa Claus. The trees stood crystallized by the subzero weather. Clouds of steam issued from our mouths. There was a pale brightness in the air, and the setting sun left behind it a radiant, slowly receding rim of reds, from the deepest purple to the palest golden-orange, until this, too, would be absorbed by the ordinary radiant blue of the wintry sky. The trees stood still as a forest of ice, and it seemed as if one harsh word or a piercing shout could shatter them into thousands of crystal fragments. The snow gave creaking noises, dark blue in the shadows of the trees. There was a crust on the snow, and it was Christmas Eve.

We loaded our bags and clambered in. Soft Christmas music came from the car radio, and the Rover sped almost soundlessly down the narrow, winding roads. We drove on while Eskil's steady voice told about the four-wheel drive and the high cost of gas, about roads that didn't exist and unnoticeable bumps, and about how we and the Söders would visit them on Christmas Day. Eskil was wearing an Icelandic sweater that smelled of oil. Wet snow had frozen into hard pearls on my mittens. I put them against my face, breathed through them. The rearview mirror was misted over. Eskil sat as if he were driving a tractor, with gentle motions. Snow fell from the low fir branches, and to each side, the storybook forest looked mysterious and dark, weighted with snow and silence.

This was the first Christmas I had ever celebrated at someone else's house, out in the country. It all began when Söder wrote Dad:

"Dear friend, now Christmas is upon us and Nora and I long to see you out here. There's peace under the roof and an open horizon to the south. Gerda and Marvin are coming—and so should you, too! We'll arrange accommodations at Eskil Ekholm's, but celebrate Christmas with us. Please come!

"With greetings from the parrot, Nora and Otto Söder."

I was so happy it hurt. We felt giddy. How? Could we go off? Cancel our Christmas Day coffee at Aunt Eva's? Break all our familiar, homey customs and leave our tree bare, dark, and lonely on Christmas Eve? Of course, said Mom. But we must be able to contribute, take some food along.

"Yes! We can!"

Dad answered the very same day Söder's letter came. And I hardly took in a word the teacher said that whole week before the Christmas holidays began.

Voices murmured, snowballs flew like loud shouts through the air; frost etched stars on the damp windowpanes of the classrooms. It was dark when we walked to school, and dark when we went home. Everywhere, in all the corridors and also at home, in the front hall, there were piles of winter clothes, sweaters, ski boots, mittens, long scarves. And wind swept more snow in from the ocean. Gray days turned the weather milder, and then sparrows flew like the wind among the dark shrubs. And now, finally, the woods, the clearings, the summer roads in snow and silence, the bend in the road up toward the bay, the smell from the cow barn and the low, red, rambling building with its seven windows, each window lit from within like a greeting and a promise of happy Christmas to those of us from the city.

As soon as we entered the vestibule with its spruce boughs decorating the stairs, we were greeted by the scent of freshly baked coffee cake. After we had settled into the guest room, with its double bed and an extra bed for me, the blue-flowered wallpaper, white curtains, and cheerful carpets, we sat down together in the room where Brita served us coffee. We sat at a long table made of two wide oak boards, bright from the wear and tear of years. The begonias bloomed on the windowsills. The stove was freshly whitewashed, and while our conversation ran along its own peaceful grooves, the movement of the old wall clock ratcheted forward minute after minute, whirred and struck its hours and half hours. And everything out there, the purity and hospitality, seemed to make the day specially meaningful; no loudspeakers shrieked their syrupy Christmas carols; there was no hurrying, no scurrying people, nor so many facing Christmas fearfully alone. Over in the corner stood the spruce Eskil had chopped down that very morning, spreading its fresh scent. It was dark green with strong, full branches and thick needles, just as it should be. Marvin and Gerda had already driven down to Paradise.

"Söder hasn't much pep. But still he's in a wonderfully cheerful mood. His heart is failing, we'd better face it."

"He'll see this Christmas, and that's good," said Brita Ekholm.

Then she fastened her brown-gingerbread eyes on me and asked,

"This will be a very different kind of Christmas for all of you, won't it?"

I nodded. A different Christmas! I wanted to jump up and run out, rush off through the woods, and then, later, out of breath, let myself fall and feel the chill, clean snow against my mouth and eyebrows.

We all got up, loaded our things on the long sled that Eskil pulled out of the carpentry workshop, and started off toward Paradise. A weak wind blew off the sea. The flaming red border in the west had narrowed to a thin glow. The woods and fields deepened into blue. A fringe of clouds hung heavy with snow. Dad and I pushed, the snow squeaked, and on the hillside down to the yellow cottage we clung to the sled, each with one foot on a protruding part of the runner and the other like a snow-spraying brake behind us.

Here, too, we were greeted by light in the windows. Nora came running out of the vestibule and threw her arms around my neck, her cheek burning against my cold skin: "Come in! Come in! Oh, how we've been waiting for you!"

"We have, too! You can't imagine!"

We stamped the snow off our boots and entered the spruce-scented, fruit-scented cottage.

Christmas Eve

We sat around the table laid for Christmas dinner. Candles glittered in the old green-and-brown bottles. Gerda had prepared everything ahead of time in the kitchen with Nora. Marvin held up a ship model in a bottle in front of the three-branched candlestick:

"It's sailing straight ahead. Look!"

He moved the bottle backward and forward, and Söder followed the movements with his eyes from his creaking rocking chair. Söder's spruce decorated with red apples stood in the corner by the captain's bridge.

"Marvin chose it," said Nora. "It's not easy when they all look like snowdrifts. You have to shake life into them, poor things."

"I looked and looked," said Marvin. "But this was the neatest and fullest and strongest. It could carry all of Christmas, everything! So I brought it home."

He put his bottle down carefully. He rested his hands on his knees, his eyes glowed happily. I thought: He belongs here, he's at home. And it didn't feel good to think about the city, his kitchen alcove, his life in the paper warehouse, where he stood sorting hour after hour.

My eyes searched out the dark form of Bow Island. But still, how lonesome and hard it must be to live there, through all the gray days, through storms and rainy weather.

"Dinner's ready," announced Gerda. "This is the last dish. Now we can begin!"

Potatoes and herring were on the table, and beets and a Christmas galantine and liver paste and a little keg of anchovies. And, impressive in the center, stood the Christmas ham with its shield of mustard and crusty bread crumbs, brown and juicy. There was beer in tankards and milk for those who wished it. Söder ceremoniously measured out Christmas drinks for the adults from an old carafe decorated with an ornamental floral border. I smiled at Nora and she smiled back. The steaming platter of potatoes, the kind grown in sandy soil, mealy and fresh, was passed from hand to hand. The keg of anchovies spread its spicy scent like a greeting from the sea and sun, and the marinated herring melted on the tongue. Söder told about his Christmases in foreign lands, in the days when sailing ships left Mariehamn bound for Australia. Our voices mingled, rose and fell, happy and thoughtful; sometimes I just had to sit quietly and listen to all of us and enjoy the fact that we were all together. Marvin sat silently, too, but I could see how happy he was, how eagerly he passed the platters; how he observed, listened.

When dinner was over, Söder said, "We thank you, the unseen, for your peace."

I didn't really understand his words, but they stuck in my mind as if they were the answer to an unspoken question.

And Dad said, "Thank you all. Here we are in Paradise."

No more needed to be said. We helped clear the dishes and then settled down around the drop-leaf table by the window overlooking the ocean. Söder glanced at Gerda and she brought out his big old Bible and read the Christmas gospel in a low, clear voice.

". . . And it came to pass in those days, that there went out a decree from Caesar Augustus, that all the world should be taxed. . . ."

We listened quietly. And after the shepherds came, we returned to the mundane; the steaming copper coffeepot was brought in and placed on the table with cups and glasses.

"I can't offer you any unusual drinks," said Söder, "but there's still some akvavit. That's been a healthy drink all my life."

"Nonsense," said Nora. "Watch out! I know you drunkards."

"Youth is determined these days," commented Söder. "Anyway, maybe you could get out the basket of Christmas presents."

Then we all, marveling, exchanged gifts, lovingly given and received. We stood up as each gift was given. No mountain of paper, no exhausting fervor. What perhaps pleased me most was a miniature fishing smack from Nora and Söder. It had a real frame hull with decks of lighter wood and a rowboat with oars secured to the deck. It felt as if I were holding a big shell in my hand. Tears came to my eyes, I brushed them away with the sleeve of my sweater. And from Marvin I got a fishnet that he had knotted very competently, and I exclaimed,

"Oh, it's really fine. You did all this!"

"So you can catch all the fishes in the sea," said Marvin.

"My nets catch nothing now but snow and wind," said Söder. "That's the way it goes. A toast, everyone, and welcome once again."

He spoke rather solemnly, but it felt appropriate, as if it was right not to talk in an ordinary way. Outside in the darkness somewhere, Bow Island lay on the ice like an animal's backbone, and somewhere on Bow Island was an abandoned cottage, in which Marvin and Gerda had lived all their lives and then left. How strange it all was. How everything changed and yet remained like itself! The room and the people here, every detail, everything I had come to know a few summers ago was still there, but in another light. The fishnets cast their pattern on the ceiling, the parrot, all excited, had executed a jerky Christmas dance and now, ruffling his neck feathers, was sounding forth his familiar "Rrrroaaaaa! Rrrrroaaaa!" Nora's corner was the same as before, but we were different. We had changed.

Söder sucked on his empty pipe—his "pacifier," as he called it—and said,

"We really weren't meant to live in luxury. When people have really a lot, they only want more and get swelled up with power."

Gerda held her saucer full of coffee balanced on her fingers like a tray; she blew on it and said,

"Poverty is hellish. You go beyond a borderline which is invisible but which does exist and you lose your human value."

But Marvin leaned toward Gerda and asked,

"Read 'Star Eye'! Please!"

"It's my turn," said Nora. "I keep books by Topelius over in my corner. I'll go get him."

She came back with the dark-green volume with the name Zacharias Topelius printed in gold letters on the cover.

" 'Once upon a time there was a little infant, lying in a snowdrift. Why was it lying in a snowdrift?—' "

"Because it was lost!" shouted Marvin.

" 'This was on Christmas Eve. The old Lappish man was driving his reindeer over the lonely, dreary hills, and the old Lappish woman followed after with her reindeer. The snow glittered, the northern lights snapped and sparkled, and the stars shone brightly in the heavens. . . .' "

As we listened, the candle flames lengthened slowly, flickering. We listened to the wintry tale of the foundling with the strange eyes which could see into the human heart and quell storms and which, on Christmas Night, could even see as far as the veil before God's invisible throne; the story of Star Eye, who disappeared, but who is still near us and can read our thoughts. I was hearing it for the first time, but Marvin knew it by heart. He sat still, his lips moving.

When Nora finished, he said,

"I've seen her. Somewhere here. Not in the city."

"Of course you've seen her," said Nora. "If anyone knows her, it would be you. That's the way it is, and just as it should be."

We burst into laughter. Resolute Nora was like a brisk wind whenever things got too tranquil. And when we stood up to leave, we were all cheerful. We let our eyes grow accustomed to the snow-bright night. It was as if the earth were quietly glowing from within. The universe was silent and the silence was immense. On the hill toward Vik, Dad stopped to say,

"We'll always remember this Christmas, won't we?"

But it wasn't a question. He didn't need to ask. We looked back. The light from Paradise shone from between the tree trunks. The sky had cleared, and through the sharp, dry air a cow could be heard mooing in the barn, friendly, making a long, drawn-out call. In front of Eskil's door we stamped off the snow and then entered a new warmth.

Winning and Losing

We peeled off our layers of winter clothes, one after the other. One by one we came out, thin and naked, and ran under the showers. We shrieked and splashed; someone turned on icy water, others wrestled. Rubberhead took his time soaping his body. It was hairy. The sauna was burning hot, some heroes threw water on the stones, small kids made their way out, couldn't even sit on the lowest benches. We pulled on our swimming trunks and walked out into the chilly swimming-pool hall. The smell of chlorine hit us, the water shimmered greenly with black, trembling wave lines along the bottom.

We divided at once into two teams for relay races. Those who weren't included sat on the bench, watching. I felt my heart pound. I was the Olympic winner and the eternal loser. We drew lots for the order in which we'd swim. I wanted to be one of the first but I came last, had to swim the last lap.

Outside the big glass windows, the January landscape spread out frozen and gray. It was all steamed over. A shrill whistle pierced the damp air. The first boys got into position. The lanes were empty. Rubber-head held his chronometer in one hand, raised the other. "Go!"

They dove in, gliding like shadows, surfaced, and plunged on, some slowly, surely, some with quicker strokes. Our class lined the sides of the pool, shouting. They turned with a swift somersault, headed back.

I had practiced the crawl all autumn but wasn't very good at turning. When I forced myself, I got winded, swallowed water, made a lot of unnecessary motions. The point was to hit a fast rhythm that was also calm and steady. I could achieve it now and then, but it fell apart in swimming matches. For a moment, while waiting my turn, I had the sense that all the shouting, the whole show, was meaningless. And through my mind, like the bodies in the water, glided the image of a mild summer day and myself, floating, my arms outspread, motionless, on the water's surface, with summer clouds above me. . . .

It was my turn. We were leading by a couple of meters; that was all, but enough. When Frederick's hands made contact, I plunged in, let myself glide, while my heart pounded, thundering in my ears. Now! I surfaced, fast, too fast, I hardly saw the dark head in the lane beside me; I forced myself, tried to get my breath, movements, everything to fit. The other end of the pool came toward me too fast; still twenty-five meters to go; this time I got the somersault right; I kicked, suddenly felt: I'm free! I'm not competing! I'm gliding, like a bird, in my own body. I don't care about winning! It was like entering into another, more flexible, easier kind of breathing, in which I myself chose whether or not to accelerate. It worked. It worked to swim faster, in *that* rhythm. I heard them shout, as if from far, far away: "Johnny!"

When I touched the end of the pool, I knew that I had won, as if I'd won twice. First, when I won my own rhythm. The second time wasn't important.

We shook hands. I was pounded on the back. I, who otherwise never excelled; I, to whom no one really paid much attention; I, who mostly walked by myself—now I was accepted. Was it that simple—just to win?

They would forget in the next echoing basketball hour. At the next vault of the horse, the next hard, fast, goal-conscious cuff from Rubberhead, they would stand around grinning, laughing, choosing, comparing. Who won? Who was the best? Who was the fastest, the cleverest, the best in the gang? Who was the leader? Was there anyone who was not following?

While I slowly got dressed again, I felt both happy and empty. Frederick said, "Hey, damn it, you look as if you'd lost. We won! We won!"

He stretched out his arms and foolishly jogged in place, mouthing a triumphant, "Yippee!"

"Out! Out!" they usually shouted in basketball. Not to mention soccer matches—a test of strength. Tests. Endless sequences of tests, examinations, papers added to papers, reports to reports. And somewhere, now, in a basement, Marvin was sorting paper. Maybe the very pages that would be handed to us one day in May, all printed, on the last day of school.

I stopped outside the swimming-pool hall, breathed

in the clear, raw air, the heavy ozone. The woods were brittle with frost, waiting to become paper. If only a wind could whirl up all the paper into the sky like birds, and heave it out, cloud-high, over the ocean! I felt uneasy, furious in a way I couldn't explain. There were too many set, regimented lanes, too many corridors, too many doors, plans, schedules everywhere. Would the spring never come? Sometimes I didn't hear what Dad and Mom said to me, sometimes I wasn't thinking about anything. I'd sit with Marvin and wish I were somewhere else. I might hang around with Frederick for hours listening to pop music and get nothing out of it. I'd come home late and Mom would be angry because I hadn't phoned to tell her where I was. I was nowhere. The worst was when books turned into a jumble of words strung one after another. I listened impatiently to Marvin's halting descriptions of what he had done or his slow spelling.

When I came home, there was a slip of paper inside the door, hopefully confident, written in big capital letters:

DON'T COME IF YOU DON'T WANT TO. MARVIN

I held the paper, felt it like a jab in my throat, as if something broke up inside me. I had got very far away, not only from Bow Island and Paradise but also from home. There was nothing I could do about it. And Marvin suspected this; he was offering me his hand with this laboriously folded slip of paper. It said, Maybe you've forgotten me. I'm not forcing you to remember.

I hadn't seen him for a week—no, two.

"Is that you, Johan?" Mom shouted from the kitchen.

"Yes!" I shouted back. "I'm dashing over to see Marvin for a while!"

"We're eating in an hour."

"Good!"

I ran down the stairs, across the yard, rang the bell loudly.

"Look who's here! Johan!" said Gerda. She wiped her hands on her apron.

"Is Marvin home?"

"He's asleep. But he'll wake soon. Come in!"

I stood in the warm, dim light of their narrow dark room. It was always tidy and clean. The yellow table-cloth glowed like a sun.

"Sit down."

Gerda looked at me, and I felt embarrassed. I had to say something.

"How's your job?"

"Well, if your back gets bent and crooked, your soul does, too, just as easily," said Gerda. She smiled slightly. "It's mostly the routine that's killing. Otherwise I wouldn't complain. We haven't seen you for a while. You have a lot to do in school."

I shook my head. "No. Not especially."

"What is it? Marvin misses you. Did you quarrel?"

"No, not at all. It's just—just that I don't feel at home anywhere. I—I'd like to do something, something different. Something I could enjoy. We had relay races today and our team won. I noticed that the winning wasn't important. But for a moment then I felt that I was getting ahead the way I wanted to, floating just like last summer. I can't explain."

Gerda sat quietly. Then she said,

"Yes. Maybe it's because we don't get a chance to be truly satisfied. So then we really do begin to stoop and don't straighten up again. Except Marvin. He doesn't change, not much. He's happy with so little, and yet— He works so hard that he has to lie down and rest when he comes home. The warehouse boss says that he doesn't see or hear, he gets so involved in his work, as if it were a matter of life and death."

She paused, then added,

"Maybe it is."

"What if I took him to the movies or something?"

"That would be just fine. I rarely can, we put aside every penny we can spare, and that's not much. Most of it goes for rent and food. Sometimes it seems as if the darkness will never lighten."

She looked out through the narrow window toward the walls across the court. "As if the sun will never reach here."

Then she straightened up, tapped her forehead, and smiled. "So we have to try to be the sunlight ourselves, don't we?"

"We're pretty good suns!"

We smiled at each other, then laughed again over how we had tramped down into that gray marsh where you can't see beyond your outstretched hands and, what is more, think they look awful as well. We were the gray-marsh folk always at a distance from each other, who get ourselves down and yet pull ourselves up again. Healthy we were, hungry we were not. We chewed our gray-weather gruel in our gray-weather marsh, and then one fine day we overcame it: spring in the air! Premature, just a slightly warmer sun, on this or that afternoon, water dripping from the roof, freezing again at nightfall. I wasn't the only one to see it. The trees had a slightly deeper violet veil. Not everything would turn to wood pulp. Being alone was good; being together was good. The important thing was that we could sit together at a table, and talk, and that our eyes saw, dark and light, ugly and beautiful, everything about each other.

Per

Per crossed one well-pressed trouser leg over the other and gazed at me with his clear, cool stare.

"Problems?"

Per never used unnecessary words. He had come to my school after Christmas, his father was a diplomat. He had visited many countries and knew English, French, and Polish. We weren't crazy about him—he kept to himself. But gradually and without having to put it into words, a contact had grown between him and me. We could do things together without discussing it. We'd take walks side by side, watch the same films, and Per could always give a clear summary of what he'd seen and thought. Often his opinion was also mine. To the rest of us, he always seemed to dress like a snob. We really felt like dragging him through a sewer, giving him a going over, making him "one of us." I wanted to, as well, but then again, I didn't. Was it necessary?

Per was sure about every possible topic; he never did any unnecessary work, helped if he was asked to, sometimes looked bored to death, as if he found everything childish. But he listened, observed, remembered. Geography and history were right at his fingertips.

He lived with his dad in a big home outside of town. I visited him there. There was a dark hall with stairs leading to the second floor and corridors. His room was high-ceilinged. He had books, a desk, and a camp bed right in the midst of all that heavy, elegant furniture.

"I've got used to it. I can't sleep on a soft bed."

During soccer matches, while I was still trying my hardest, running to and fro—most of the time in vain—he would be leaning against the railing.

"Running after a ball and then trying to put it in between two posts, running two seconds faster than someone else, or scrambling up the world's highest mountain only to scramble down again, leaves me cold," he said. "There are more enjoyable ways of killing time."

He said that in the locker room, loud and clear.

He didn't care what he said.

Alf flared up. He was the chairman of the school's sports club.

"Damn snob!"

Per shrugged his shoulders; he was ready, and he left. He always got dressed faster than the rest of us.

"We'll show him. We'll put him in his place. That's the only way."

Three days later a warming sun shone from a cloudless sky. It shone in puddles on the courtyard, and the air was light to breathe. Crying gulls lifted off into the wind, and down in the harbor, huge, fragmented ice floes drifted free. Windows, opened for the first time in a long while, flashed like lightning, and voices floated up like cheerful streamers. Thaw dripped, water splashed, gusts of wind bowed over the birches. Alf had just thrown the ball.

Deftly and speedily he threw the wet, muddy ball into Per's face. It happened so fast that Rubberhead didn't see it. Or did he? His first shrill whistle sounded as Per walked slowly over to Alf. He had picked up the ball and was balancing it on his fingertips. Three steps away from Alf, Per let the ball fall to the ground, caught it again with his foot, dribbled past. Alf lunged, but clumsily. Everyone was caught off guard. Per moved along fast, wiped the dirt from his face—it was as if he were alone on the field. Rubberhead's whistle blew again, but he didn't hear it, quickly made his own attack, wheeled past Frederick, rushed him, shot the ball, fast and hard, up toward the right goal corner, out of reach.

It was as if a film had stopped. Everyone stopped. Per had kicked his own goal, purposefully, fast. Rubberhead's whistling turned breathless and died.

I suddenly felt a wild joy, which rose and stuck in my throat. I watched him stroll up toward the park, and no one followed him, no one called him back. We stood staring into the strong sunlight, watching him disappear.

"Come back immediately!" shouted Rubberhead.

His voice broke like a magpie's shrill call. No one listened. The game went on, but as if both the ball and the rest of us were deflated. Alf ran around frenetically, achieved nothing, made a lot of noise like an empty barrel. We tumbled into the locker room, where silence fell. Only Alf swore, silently, to himself. When we got up to the classroom, Per was sitting there.

Alf went over to him. "You think you own the whole world. You think you know everything, including soccer. Which doesn't prevent you from being a shit and a snob. The simplest thing in the world is for you to clear out, coward!"

Per got up slowly. "Is it? Is it the simplest thing in the world? What would a mountain of flesh like you know about that?"

Alf's fist shot out, but Per caught it, twisted it swiftly, and forced Alf to bend over, slowly, soundlessly.

We stood in a circle, looking on, as always.

Alf tried to hit him with his free arm, but Per caught him in a stranglehold and pressed down until Alf lay with his face against the floor. Then Per said, breathing hard, "You have enough strength for three and the brains of an ape!"

He released him suddenly. Alf rose. They looked at each other.

Per put out his hand. "Okay. No offense. If you let me be, I'll let you be. Agreed?"

Alf turned aside, didn't look at him, sat in his seat.

Per shrugged, went and sat in his place. Only the rumble of our feet and the slamming of our desktops held their own against the heavy silence. The teacher came in and our class began. After it was over, we all walked out and left Per. He stood in an empty room.

I wanted to go over to him, shake him, talk with him. I avoided it, like a coward. I took my books and left. I felt his silence like a blow in the back.

He was left alone after that. He came and went equally silently. In every test he distinguished himself. I knew that he was studying to enter the next class. He skipped from ours; from the very start he had always been beyond us. A few terms later, he disappeared again. I remember his dark suit, his straight white legs, his dark hair, eyes that gazed clearly, steadily, and sharply. Much later, I longed to slam him against a wall, force him to make a mistake, get him to be weak, give way, give himself away; make him strike out blindly, trip someone up, betray someone, the way we all did.

He kept his secrets to himself. Perhaps he didn't have any. Gradually I came to pity him, as you pity anyone who isn't able to change.

Gerda and Marvin

"Of course I noticed early on that Marvin was different," said Gerda. "Not in the very beginning, but later. He didn't want to learn to walk, he was slow and late learning to talk, he sat quietly most of the time and sometimes I couldn't understand what he said. It was very difficult."

Her hands rested calmly on the table as she looked out our kitchen window. It was Saturday, Marvin was at a weekend program for the retarded. We listened.

"You couldn't tell whether he understood. He would look at me, and I didn't know whether he saw me. The doctor said he was retarded and should be put in an institution. There weren't any in the district, we would have been forced to move into the city. I was very much alone because Marvin's father was at sea most of the time, and even lonelier after he died. I felt it was like autumn and foggy all the time, out there on Bow Island. Then I always needed a fog-dispersing machine, and I need it more and more now, too! But then I noticed that Marvin sort of slowly woke up and started to look around. And it was obvious to me that he saw in a way that I had never seen. He heard sounds long before I heard them, and everything made him happy. He was very slow and difficult to teach—how to dress, how to eat neatly. But eventually he could learn. He went to Solgården clinic for three weeks when he was ten, but he didn't get on there. I fetched him and met the doctors there and they were very friendly. They told me that Marvin is like a telescope, so sometimes he sees little things very close and huge, and then sometimes everything is very far away. Like a telescope. That's how Marvin sees himself."

I thought of our old opera glasses; how I could sit staring through them out over the roof at a distant perching bird or a mocking, scornful, dirty dove pacing back and forth impetuously on a window ledge or a gull with its wings outstretched on a chimney pot, absolutely still; how everything came close and yet belonged to a totally different world. Like a spy, a stranger, I sat and observed.

"He had a hard time if anyone except me ever touched him. He got frightened, and sometimes he couldn't utter a single word. Everything would just go to pieces. Sometimes I would get dead tired. But there were rewards, and they started coming more and more often. Because Marvin can listen like no one else. Where the rest of us are crooked, he is straight. Inside, he is happy—not always, but when he is, not even this backyard can kill it."

She looked up hastily, but Dad said, "We understand, it must be incredibly difficult."

"I don't want to sound ungrateful."

"I know."

"It is starting to go better now, that's true. And Marvin—he's grateful. When he says thanks for something, he means it so sincerely that you really feel wretched and false and almost hypocritical by comparison. He is the cleanest, purest person I've ever met, and that's how he gives me strength. Of course he is lonely, but less so than you'd think. He's always busy making something with his hands. He never gets sorry for himself, only things outside make him unhappy, something unjust, someone who was mean, something he saw that frightened him. He's sensitive, more sensitive than we are, almost like a barometer, the way we were as children and then maybe lost."

She sat quietly for a moment and then continued,

"Often I think—when everything weighs me down heavily—that he is the most valuable experience I've ever had. I hope that a few others who can really feel might be able to experience that, too. Then maybe we would be more full of love."

She nodded to herself, as if she heard the phrase for the first time, dared to express it—more full of love.

"So we mustn't hide him, we mustn't turn away from him, pityingly. He is the way he is, he has reached his full growth, and we are the ones who have to change. Sometimes I think that we are the peculiar ones, the ones who are off course, who sidestep and avoid things—that Marvin is the one who stands firm and close to everything basic—birds and dreams and people's thoughts. As if to show that what we believe to be fixed, certain, once and for all, something to grab hold of, is often really worthless, and that the important thing is what you have to give, not what you have or what you take, but what you give. If only we could learn from him—"

She fell silent. Through the half-open window came a breeze, a scent of spring, like hope.

The Paper Company

Someone pounded on the door a week later, someone who woke me up out of my book; my heart leaped into my throat. Someone knocked and knocked, gradually more weakly, like a heart. I heard a snuffling sound. I ran and threw open the door.

Marvin had been kneeling with his forehead pressed against the door. A package lay beside him. He was sniffling and his eyes were rolling wildly.

"Mom isn't home. Not home. Not home."

I tugged and dragged and got him into our hall.

"The package!"

I pulled it in, too. "Take it easy, Marvin. What happened?"

"Oh, oh, oh."

He wailed like a little baby, rocking in the dark. "Oh, oh. I didn't find it. Nothing. They changed all the streets. There was a dog. It wanted to bite me."

He grabbed my arm, his white face stared at me with two buttonlike eyes. "It bit. Look!"

He stretched out two strong white wrists. Not a scratch on them.

"Marvin! You're dreaming! Nothing terrible has happened."

"The boss will be angry, he'll throw me out! He comes up very close to me. He talks and talks, I can't answer."

He rocked back and forth, with his hands covering his face, and his words came out shakily, "I couldn't! I just couldn't!"

My thoughts turned to that summer, that day when Erik tried to tie Marvin up. That was just the way he was trying to worry himself free right now, working himself loose from his own knots. They were invisible. Sweat glistened on his forehead.

"I-i-it wanted to b-bite me! He shouted that it would!"

"Who?"

"The man who should have the package. It was wrong! He didn't listen, just shouted. I ran, I ran all the way."

The mail slot rattled. His eyes stared in terror. He took refuge farther down our hall. The evening paper thudded lightly onto the carpet; steps died away down the stairwell.

"It was a mistake, Marvin, the whole thing. I'll come with you. We'll go back to the warehouse together. Now blow your nose and wash your face. Come on!"

He didn't budge.

I nearly roared, "Get up!"

I dragged him out to the bathroom, handed him a

facecloth, turned on the cold water. He snuffled and snorted and peered up out of the face cloth, flaming red, his hair straggling and matted, but his eyes calmer, almost abashed. "I got scared."

"Sure, people get scared. I often get scared. I'm scared of all sorts of things. People who bang on the door and strange sounds and people who make threats and scream, and sometimes I'm scared of nothing, of something I think I saw or heard—or something someone said about me—"

I stopped talking. He certainly wouldn't get any calmer listening to what *I* was afraid of.

I said, "Someone else can deliver that package. I'll talk to your boss. Come along, now."

An icy wind was blowing through the city. A fine rain lashed us in the face. Spring was nothing more than a promise taken back. Tree trunks were dark and damp. When we walked over the Long Bridge, a heavy smell of smoke and soot struck us, mixed with the smell from the gasworks farther away.

We walked through the entry of an old yellow house, crossed the inner yard, and went down a few steps. The yard was like many others. They were everywhere, children played in them, enclosed by walls, as if in prisons. But the sign over the door was freshly painted: THE PAPER COMPANY.

The boss stood at a large metal table under a low-hanging lamp, cutting reams of paper. He pressed down a lever. His glasses caught the light as he faced us.

"Well, what is it?"

Marvin had stopped at the door, pressing himself

against it as if he wanted to disappear. The storeroom
was hot, smelled of glue and dust; not a welcoming
smell.

"I'm a friend of Marvin here. He didn't find the
address and got scared and then he came to me."

The man took his cigarette stub out of his mouth
and aimed it deftly right into a metal bucket in the
corner. "Just what I thought."

"Maybe it wasn't so smart to send him, because he
still doesn't know the city too well."

He pushed his cap with its eyeshade back, rubbed
his nose, and looked at me, rather craftily but in a
friendly way. "Even a strange bird like him has to
try his wings sooner or later, I thought. But he fell
flat. So there."

Then, after blowing his nose in the world's largest
and dirtiest handkerchief, he added, "Nothing wrong
with the boy, otherwise, if you don't expect too
much."

He shouted, "Marvin!"

Marvin approached, frightened.

"I'll send someone else with the package. Okay? It
was dumb of me to send you."

"I can! I can! But I couldn't read. It was the wrong
address."

The man looked at the package, squinting, as if
peering at an insect. His face was totally round, with
a broad, friendly mouth. He said, "That damn
witch's scrawl tripped you up. I should have seen that
right off. But I did explain the way you should walk.
Oh, well. Live and learn. Go on home now. See you
Monday."

He turned and went on working, mumbling softly to himself. I took Marvin's arm and we walked back; across the blustery yard, down the wide street, over the bridge. We walked in silence, with our hands deep in our jacket pockets. To each of Marvin's steps, I had to take almost two. An old man with a bottle was sitting in our entry. Marvin stopped. I tugged at him. "Come on! That's nothing to stare at."

Marvin stopped by his door. "They don't find it. They just drink and then they die."

"Find what?"

"Home. If you don't find it, you die."

Whistling shrilly, Peter cycled into the entry, braked violently in front of us, then spat on the ground and gestured with his head. "Weirdos."

Whistling again, he disappeared around the corner, leaving a crack in our conversation. Matti opened the door. "Don't just stand there, come on in."

He squeezed my arm in the vestibule. "Gerda has been very anxious. What happened? Has he—?"

"Just a misunderstanding. He made a mistake with a package."

"Mistake! Was the address wrong or couldn't he find it?"

"I don't really know. The address was probably wrong."

"Don't know. There's a big difference."

"Is there?"

He let go of my arm, changed to a smile, walked into the living room. "The lost son is restored."

The lost son sat on the edge of his bed in the alcove behind the kitchen with a mug of hot, milky coffee in his fist. Gerda stroked his hair with her red, swollen hand. "Glad you're here. Stay awhile, Johan."

Marvin handed over his empty cup, then lay down full-length on his bed and shut his eyes. He said to himself,

"I really can. If no one frightens me. Then I can."

He was silent. Gerda covered him with a blanket. Matti stood by the door; I walked past him.

"You won't stay?"

"He's sleeping. But I'll come back."

Matti put his hand on Gerda's shoulder. It was as if he touched *me*; it felt unpleasant. I walked out, quietly closing the door behind me. It was blowing hard; the old man with the bottle had disappeared. I didn't feel at home anywhere. I heard someone crying on the stairs. My footsteps echoed. The sound stopped. Ulla Lehto sat on the stairs between the first and second floors.

"What happened?"

"I was over with Minna on the stairs to C entry, and when I walked down someone grabbed me. It was dark, I struggled free—"

"Could you see who it was?"

She looked at me. Then she shook her head as if she wanted to convince herself that she didn't know. She got up and we walked together. I said,

"Perhaps you should call the police."

"No!"

She stopped at our door, stared at me with her thin, spotty red face and her almost-white hair. "You mustn't tell anyone!"

"Why not?"

"There'll only be trouble at home. Dad and Mom fight all the time and then he starts on me. Promise!"

Two anxious eyes filled her face.

"I promise."

She disappeared up the stairs and I went in to Dad and Mom, to the stillness, the peace, the books, the warm red blanket I could pull over my head, the sleep—home to myself, to my room, my things, to the questions, the answers, home.

Söder

The steel-and-glass building mirrored the evening sky. Every window shone. It was like an enormous anthill full of sick ants. They ran down the corridors or shuffled about. Stretchers rolled by and disappeared around corners. A gigantic ivy plant sucked in germs on the information desk. People were lined up in front of the cigarette machine. The girl in a starched uniform wore her hair like Madame Pompadour, with a white napkin on top of it all. She raised her eyebrows.

"Section Sixty-four, sixth floor. Elevator to the right."

I thanked her and made my way to the row of express elevators in the hospital skyscraper. I was holding a bouquet of flowers from Mom and Dad. It felt as if it were stuck to my arm. I hadn't visited a hospital in ages.

Otto Söder had asked me to come. He had sent word by way of Nora that he wanted to talk with me.

He was in for a few days' observation. Why did he want to see me?

"He wants to talk with you alone," said Nora. "Don't be frightened, he's shrunk like an old lemon. We'll all get that way if we live long enough and keep our health. But he's just as stubborn as before, really tough and stubborn, so it won't be easy for them to take his life away from him."

"Who do you mean?"

"Oh, the whitecoats, of course. They poke and prod, and the younger they are, the more questions they ask. When I was down with appendicitis, a whole crowd of them came and asked what I needed. Peace and quiet and no stupid questions, I told them. They grinned like wolves."

"Can I take anything with me?"

"Nothing. 'Bye now. And remember, don't be scared."

With a whine, the elevator slung me upward, stopping abruptly like a punch in the stomach. From up there you could see the city like a glimmering pattern of lights, and the bright spring sky stretched a long, narrow cloud like a weightless dark feather over the darkening houses.

Söder lay under the big white bedclothes. I almost didn't recognize him. His cheeks had become sunken, his hands stuck out from the sleeves of the hospital pajamas, so thin and long. But his clear eyes glittered, noticing everything.

"Good you came. Not much fun for a boy like you."

"Dad and Mom send greetings. Here are some flowers."

"Give them to the nurse so she can put them in a vase. It's nice of you, but not necessary. I don't need anything, I just accept it. But I asked you to come so I could give you something."

There were curtain partitions between each of the three beds. Söder pointed to his night table. The stubble of his beard glinted like silver. "Open that drawer. There's a case inside I want you to take."

I found a long, black-leather case, which I handed to him. He had difficulty turning his head and difficulty opening the lock.

Inside lay a telescope in black leather and brass, the kind you pull to lengthen, like the ones Marvin and I had seen in the books about old sailing ships.

Söder said, "This is for you. Nora gets the rest, but this is for you. I want to give it to you now, to make sure you have it. You can see really far with it, maybe even see something invisible."

I looked down at the telescope in my arms and had trouble finding words.

"Thanks, Uncle Otto."

And he, with his eyes closed, said, "Have I turned into your uncle now?"

"It happened by itself. How do you feel?"

"It happens by itself. Faster, slower. Sometimes so fast you can't feel anything."

I sat there silently for a while. He opened his eyes, looked at me. "You know you can go, boy. I know you're pleased and you'll take good care of it. I've seen a lot with it."

"Remember Christmas Eve?" I asked. "You said something when we'd finished eating. It was a prayer.

I didn't understand it. 'We thank you, the unseen, for your peace.' "

His eyes looked right into mine. "What you see and what you can put your hands on, all that is created naturally—no God has been in on that. That's a lot of nonsense. Facts are facts, ask Nora."

He lay there quietly for a second. His hair was still thick, but pure white. I had to lean forward to hear better.

"But what we think and dream, what we see and create out of nothing, and what we communicate when we are silent—the unseen, the invisible, everything invisible, now that has been given to us by something invisible. The most beautiful."

He murmured, "Must be someone—someone serene—"

He looked at me, grabbed my hand, held me by the wrist, hard. He seemed powerfully moved. I was scared. But then his gaze grew clear again, he released his grasp, smiled slightly at me. "Go now. Maybe we won't see each other again. Then you'll know that I was happy when you saw me. You be happy, too, about everything you see and about everything that you don't see, but can create yourself in your life. Remember: I live in Paradise."

He turned his face away, his eyes closed. I rose silently and left. I walked through the corridors, down the stairs, down the long, hard paths, out into the city and the spring. I took deep breaths; the air was still chilly. I walked all the way home, windows slipped by, and the telescope in my hand felt like a staff, a support, like a challenge or a promise: to see clearly. Headlights of passing cars blinded me, I had to keep blinking. I crossed over the big square and passed crowds of people all going their different ways, to their various goals. I sat for a short while on a park bench until I began to freeze. I stood up. It grew darker, some raindrops struck my face. I walked down by the docks and felt myself gradually becoming calmer, empty and clear, like the air.

TV Evening

"Did you know that a boy climbed up in a tree where an eagle had built its nest, and the eagle jabbed out his eyes and he fell and broke his neck?"

"No, Marvin, I didn't know that."

"Did you know that a boy got caught in a windmill and he went spinning around and then he fell right down and died and his head came off?"

"No."

"It's true. It's in my book. Did you know that a family lived in a teapot and slept in a coffeepot, but they didn't boil anything, they *lived* there."

Marvin looked first at Nora and then at me with bright, happy eyes, his hair standing up every which way, and he leaned forward. "Did you know there are wild animals that eat children?"

"There were," said Nora firmly, "but there aren't any more. Now they have food in cans."

"Little children?"

"Come now, you know that's not right," said Nora.

"Where do you learn all this? Some of it's smart and some of it's totally crazy."

"In an old book, and it knows. Old people know."

"An old book—that I didn't expect. Well, thank heavens for new ones! Except for stories, of course, the older the better, just like cheese. And as far as the old people are concerned, they're often completely empty-headed."

"Yes, but take Söder," I protested. "Surely he isn't empty-headed."

Nora pursed her lips tightly together. "I say no more than what's exactly right. Sure he's clever, but sometimes a head will become empty—anyone's head."

"How's he doing?"

"He can come home now. He's always better there."

"Why is your place really called Paradise?"

"What do you mean?"

I was aware that I was blushing. "I mean, who thought of it?"

"Söder, of course. He always says that it's called Paradise because it's no paradise at all. Because if everything were nice and easy we'd be bored to death and never learn a thing. It's called Paradise because it's the only place where we can feel at home and live and face our troubles. That's why it's called Paradise, because it isn't one at all. Do you see?"

"I see!" said Marvin. "Like when we lived home."

For a while, the silence was unbroken. Then Nora said, "Aren't you home here?"

Marvin answered quickly, "Did you know that there are birds which get so tired when they fly over the ocean that they have to sit down on ferry boats and you can pick them up in your hands and hold them, like this?"

He cupped his hands, looked down at them, not at us.

"And then they fly up again, like the gull—you remember, Marvin," I said.

He nodded.

He said with great effort, "Did you know? Did you know that there are pigs that can count and learn letters? They learn with their snouts. They like to be clean. It's people who make them dirty."

"No, I didn't know," Nora and I shouted almost simultaneously as if to break the silence.

Dad knocked on the door. "Can I come in?"

"Yes!"

He sat beside Marvin on the edge of the bed, smoothed back his thin hair, and said, "Ugh, what a day. If you've sat on the same chair for twenty years, you feel like a chair yourself, a chair that anyone can sit on."

"Then you have four legs," said Marvin. "Harry Vestergård, he walks on all fours, he crawled down to the water and tried to drink it. He said he ran on alcohol."

"You really know a lot," said Dad, looking happier right away.

"I've read. Gerda has read to me, and then I read it after her. And then I tell it. Then it is really good because you do it yourself."

Marvin slapped his knee and asked, "Can I watch TV?"

We all watched.

We saw six men behind a long table and a lot of other people in a big room shouting at them, and a sharp-nosed man directing the ones who were shouting and interrupting the ones who wanted to answer.

"He's mean," said Nora. "Take him away."

We switched channels.

We saw two men in long underwear dancing. Now and then, they'd take a high leap. A girl in a very short skirt came out of a little cottage and danced with one of the men while the other waved his arms. She passed out in the first man's arms and he carried her over his shoulder back into the cottage. Then a king and a queen and a whole bunch of people came on. Another man started dancing wildly.

"They have the itch," said Marvin. "They're jumping and hopping." He leaned forward with interest.

They all got tangled up with each other. The girl in the cottage couldn't decide whom she wanted to dance with, and the guys struck their foreheads with their hands, and finally she fell down and died. Then one of the men went completely wild and crazy. Taking huge leaps, he disappeared off into the forest.

"Like the Norråker bull when he's really mean," said Nora.

Dad blew his nose, his eyes wet with laughter.

The picture disappeared, and a fat lady sang about a detergent. Then came ads about deodorants, gas, and coffee. Then the picture changed, and the woods returned with their straggly trees.

The girl in tulle jumped up out of a grave, and one of her fiancés came alone furtively. He was completely inconsolable. A girl in white suddenly rushed across the screen, high up in the air from right to left, and vanished. The man and the girl from the grave danced about in a confused way, they bent this way and that, and at last he lifted her up in his arms, straight up.

"Now he'll dump her," said Marvin. "When Edla scolds Harry, he dumps her. He lifts her high up in the air, and then he dumps her on the ground so she gets a nosebleed. That was in midsummer. But this is done better."

I couldn't hold myself back. I started laughing; tears streamed, my stomach hurt. I laughed so hard that I couldn't see the picture.

Marvin was laughing, too. "They don't know how funny they are."

The girl went dead again, she swooned and the picture died out, too. Next came a pudgy, quarrelsome guy with a checked vest who talked about capitalist society.

On the other channel, the sharp-nosed man pointed at a speaker who got up and took out a paper. He talked about the treachery of the citizens.

"Is there anything else?"

"We can try the Eastern channel."

The picture was snowy. A chorus in folk costumes sang, swaying as if in a storm, but we couldn't hear a sound. Dad turned it off, the picture got tiny, then vanished. It was mercifully still and cozy.

We went out into the kitchen and the aroma of coffee.

"They threaten us every day with cutting back,

economizing, layoffs, whatever they call it," Gerda was saying. "The old machine won't cope. My hands get like hard knots, like crusty old ends of bread."

"They are so gentle," said Marvin, wrapping his arms around Gerda's shoulders.

"Oh, Marvin! If only I could get used to it. But we have Bow Island with us wherever we go. I know we couldn't go on out there, it was impossible."

A violent screeching came from the yard; a group of gulls lifted off from the dark asphalt, white against the twilight, shrieking and wailing away.

"They follow the garbage cans. They go a long way inland," said Nora. "When I came into town they were sitting on the piles of coal like mushrooms. City gulls."

We sat there chatting, heard cars braking in the distance, an ambulance, doors closing on the stairs. I belonged here, with the city gulls, on the coal piles, in three rooms and a kitchen, in backyards, here in town. I looked at the others sitting there: Dad with his deeply lined face, Mom looking serious, Gerda, Nora, Marvin, all so much the way I knew them, as I saw them. And suddenly it seemed to me that I was alone, sitting with utter strangers.

Twelve Steps

Marvin hunched over, his face contorted with effort. Shadows from the birch tree in the yard moved over him like soot. Silence fell along the course. Then he took off, astoundingly fast. He jumped away from the wood marker so fast that it flew up. He threw himself into the spring air, one step, two steps, three—went on like a kangaroo, blind and deaf to the shouts and whistles. He went on in his violent battle against the intractable earth, as if it wanted to pull him down again; he went even further, to where the yard ended and a wall stopped him just when he was about to swing up, take flight, perhaps sail away on the updraft out over the ocean, setting his course for Bow Island.

They shrieked with laughter, pointed, held their stomachs.

"Twelve steps!"

"The world's best at twelve steps!"

"Crazy loon!"

"What style!"

Marvin stood way off there, in the shadow of the wall. He dried the sweat on his forehead, came over smiling uncertainly.

"You're crazy," someone shouted from the gang.

"He's fantastic!" shouted a little boy. And he rang the bell on his bicycle wildly.

"Do it again!"

"Yes, we want him to do it again!"

They grabbed hold of him like ants on a pine needle and began dragging him toward the starting line. He didn't really defend himself. He let them pull him, a stiff smile on his face, his eyes frozen.

They put him in position, turned him facing the course—clearly drawn chalk lines on the gray asphalt.

"Jump!"

"Get going!"

"Idiot!"

"Rah, rah!"

"Remember, *three* steps."

"No, twelve!"

"Try to jump over the wall!"

Peter, who had been leaning against the wall of the house, sauntered over. He had a match in his mouth; it pointed up and down. He took it out of his mouth slowly and said, while studying Marvin from top to toe, "He doesn't understand anything. No point having him with us."

He moved his hand in front of Marvin's face, as if he were blind.

Marvin stood stock-still, following the hand with his eyes.

"City idiot!"

He said it calmly, in a friendly tone, but stood as if he might suddenly throw himself upon Peter.

"Oh, let him be!"

"He hasn't done anything!"

"He's okay."

Marvin took a step to pass Peter, but Peter quickly put himself in the way. Marvin took another step to the other side. Peter danced in front of him, as if playing with him.

Marvin stopped, with his head lowered, breathing heavily.

"Don't you want to go home to Mommy? It's only a couple of yards. You don't have to jump twelve steps, just walk. Well? What about it?"

I came into the backyard, dazzled by the sunlight, just at this point. I saw how Marvin went right for Peter, as if he were blind, as if Peter didn't exist. Their bodies locked together wildly. Peter grabbed his arm, at the same time punching his right hand into Marvin's face. Marvin wept, his face became contorted, he escaped from Peter's grasp, lifted him up into the air. Everything fell dead still. Peter kicked with his legs, with his knees, but it was as if Marvin were without feeling, a stone, a stone cross. He carried the gasping Peter over to the back wall, propped him up against it, and let him slide down.

While Peter slowly got on all fours and started scrambling to his feet, Marvin turned and walked away. He passed close by me, like a sleepwalker. I tried to grab his arm.

"Marvin!"

He went to his door in the entry, knocked, stood with his hands on the door, his head hanging down.

"You devil, you'll pay for this!" shouted Peter, but his voice broke.

The door was opened, shut again.

An unsettled wind blew, a window slammed and flashed in the spring sunlight. Peter got up, didn't look around. He brushed off his trousers with his hands, slowly, laboriously. Then he straightened up, screaming as loudly as he could, with his head far back, his face red and full of hatred, "He ought to be reported! He's crazy! Just wait!"

Something welled up inside me, my vision darkened, bright pricklings of light danced there, and hearing my voice in falsetto, I shouted back, "It's your own fault, coward!"

I would have liked to back away, into the wall, into the wall of the house, invisible. I felt the taste of blood on my lips. My body stiffened, prepared to defend myself. He came at me with bent fists, flung himself at me. Instinctively, I threw myself to one side. He caught my arm; we both slammed down on the asphalt while I thought, "Now, now, now it's coming! Now it's coming!"

I scarcely heard the shrieking ring of kids. I managed to get him on his back, pummeled and pummeled while I half-cried, "Damn you, damn you, damn you." Sweat poured down into my eyes.

Something tore at me, pulled us apart: Gerda.

"I will not have blood drawn for Marvin's sake."

Hers was a cry of need.

She looked around. "It's not his fault that he was hurt when he was born. And you, you could help him. But what do you do? You shouldn't throw stones at a cripple! You shouldn't throw stones at someone blind or lame. Well, should you? Should you? But you pick on him. And you, most of all, you should have known better."

She looked at Peter. Her hair flew, her cheekbones stood out, her face was glowing.

Then she let her arms fall to her sides, and she turned to me. "Come home with me."

We walked into the entry without looking back. I supported her as if she were mourning or very old. The dark wind buffeted us, cold on my hot face.

A voice, shrill as a bird's, screamed, "Marvin won!"

The others followed, as if they wanted to rout the wind. "Marvin won!"

While she fumbled for her key, she said slowly, "No one won. No one."

Alone

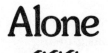

While the last weeks of school creaked by in endless classes, endless tests, and while spring like a shimmer and a sunbeam stood outside the schoolroom windows, I submerged myself in work—homework, books, notes, into anything that would protect me from myself. I didn't think about myself; I tried to shove away the image of Marvin, but never really could.

I walked down empty, blustery streets; I looked at the brightly displayed stalls full of fruit and fish in the square. I squeezed into crowds, strolled out around town with friends; came home, didn't listen, seldom answered, went to my room, read. I gazed out over the familiar roofs, the swaying chimney-pot covers. Somewhere the ocean lay like a mighty sky-blue shield; the wind scattered birds over the city, and the old houses faced into the sunlight with blind windows, looking grubby.

We worked on Saturdays, too, to make up for the holidays, and on Saturday evenings I slumped in front of the TV, slept half-dead through most of Sunday, seldom went out. The teachers seemed equally strained and drawn, as tired as we were. Occasionally it would suddenly grow dark outside and a violent rain would strike the windows. I pulled down my yellow shades, lit my lamp, held my head in my hands. And then a calm would come over me, in which almost everything felt like unimportant rubbish fit only to dispense with, to shove aside.

Sometimes I sat with Marvin, and then I'd feel calm. I'd hear Matti talking with Gerda in a low voice, sometimes upset, about strike notices, about his childhood, about going into debt for food, the constant fear that there wouldn't be enough money. A look of hate came into his eyes when he thought about his childhood. He had been hungry most of the time. He worked hard, he'd always worked hard. He looked at me as if I were to blame for his hunger. I thought about quarreling at home—it did happen, but seldom—and how I sat behind the closed door those times and heard them: they were blamed, punished, taxed; they were being pinched on all sides; food prices rose; the rent went up; the car had been sold long ago; Dad got nothing more than a percentage raise; they scarcely ever went to the theater, seldom to the movies, never to a restaurant; and their circle of friends wasn't very big.

Marvin lay on his bed, slowly spelling out *Robinson Crusoe*, an abridgment in large type. I felt like someone who had to go in between, who was always in between, who could perhaps serve as an intermediary but didn't want to, didn't have it in me.

I walked alone in the evenings, to find an unobstructed view of the ocean; I wanted to be left in peace. I watched trashy TV programs, endless shooting cowboys, moving mouths, discussions, and sometimes a landscape with red birds, a sea with fish like bright screens turned toward an invisible light and then suddenly vanishing. Seldom a face that spoke to me, that got to me. I longed for them to talk to me, Dad and Mom most of all, and yet at the same time I didn't want them to.

Did Marvin ever feel like that? He looked at me with his bright, friendly eyes. But we stood at a distance from each other. I had read three pages of a book I was holding, but I didn't remember a single word. Sometimes I dreamed I was in other countries, dreamed myself on Robinson's island or Narnia; sometimes, stubbornly, I followed the trail to California, through all the grapes of wrath. I had found that one on the shelf; it looked thick enough to challenge me. I wanted to be challenged; I wanted to live in peace. Sometimes I thought of Söder's words that Christmas Eve when everything was soft with snow, glimmeringly light, joyous and calm. About the unseen and serenity. Then Nora's firm round owl face would intervene with her voice, her words about Paradise. What had she said? Something about how if everything were just fine we would be bored to death. But what if nothing were good, nothing at all, then what? If someone cried on the stairwell so that I could hear it through my door? I walked down the quiet steps, the spring rain fell, the black asphalt shone, windows lit up. Mine was dark.

Högholmen Zoo

"We're descended from them. However red their rumps are," said Nora, staring with interest at the apes, which returned her gaze in a friendly way. They preened themselves, carried their young around their necks, swung swiftly among a few dried-out branches.

Marvin drew back. "They are in prison."

"Yes, they are locked in. All of them are locked in. That's why they're kept on an island. They can't fly."

"They can swim."

"The ones that can swim have walls around them. Swimming pools."

Marvin was holding a picture book of animals. He said, "Mom can read to us and they'll listen."

"The animals? Once I read *Peter Rabbit* to my rabbit and the next day he was dead. So she'd better watch out."

"When someone reads, the animals listen, the ones with horns," said Marvin. "They're like antennae. They catch the sounds we don't hear. Sometimes they don't need horns, they hear anyway. They hear with their skin and with their eyes. They can go every-where."

Somewhere far off a lion agreed with a muted roar. A flamingo slowly bent its snakelike neck, put its foot down carefully, as if the ground were burning hot. It was as if Marvin himself listened with his skin and eyes. He was the one telling us things, and even Nora, the wise old owl, listened.

"Bats fly in the dark, but the dark doesn't bother them. They know where the trees are, where the walls are. They are like sparks, they fly so fast. They're si-lent, but they sing all the time, we just don't hear it. Everywhere there's some animal that can't talk, but that hears more than we do. They don't want to talk. And birds see fishes under the water and worms in the ground. They see us, too."

Marvin became excited; his hair fell over his fore-head. People looked at him as they passed by. His hands gestured; he couldn't keep still; he had to move about, sidestep, stop again.

"Wouldn't you like to sit down, Marvin?" Gerda asked. She was pale; she'd lost weight. A brown beret covered her dark hair.

"Birds fly away and always get to where they are going," said Marvin. "They find the same tree and the same grass and the same sea. Dolphins talk to each other. They want to help, they're never mean."

"Our parrot can bite your finger so hard that you bleed," Nora remarked. "So there are stupid animals, too. But they don't get any nicer in cages, you can be sure of that. So watch out that you don't get nipped."

"They're caught, they can't move," said Marvin. "They'll die in the cages."

"Oh, no, they're looked after," said Nora.

Marvin stared fascinated by the flamingo. "They have legs like reeds. They are a cloud on a reed."

We made our way under the cool, tall trees. The polecat in a narrow metal cage jumped back and forth, back and forth. Marvin moved away. Matti, elegant in his leather jacket and light-colored trousers, rested a hand on Marvin's shoulder. "Yes, that poor devil isn't having a good time."

Marvin turned his back to the cage. "It wants to die!"

"Oh no, it's just bad-tempered."

But Marvin walked away from there and we all followed. It was as if he were looking for the animals that were happy. He wouldn't look at the big birds of prey under their roof. But he stopped near the deer enclosure: "There! There they are! Look, they're listening!"

A large buck raised his head, gazed beyond us with his shiny black eyes. Happy shouts, children's voices rose like balloons. A big white ferry boat slipped slowly by; it was as if the island were slowly gliding backward on the still surface of the ocean. We sat down on the top of the rise overlooking the wide view. Gerda took the juice bottles and sandwiches from her bag. Nora was unusually silent. She looked out over the ocean, shading her forehead with her hand. "I think I should go off early. Sure, my aunt is there, but still. . . . She carries on and climbs the walls to scrub the ceiling, she's that type. It's not calm enough, the way it should be for Söder."

She got up; she was uneasy. "No, stay where you are. I can manage just fine. There's a bus every hour."

She shook each of us by the hand. "Good-bye! Have a happy time!"

She smiled a little, saying that. Then she bounded off. I longed to call her back but couldn't, she wanted to go home. Marvin got up, staring after her. "She's scared about Söder. She heard, there're some who hear."

It was in the middle of May, a dark cloud bank approached from the west. A weak breeze moved through the treetops. We made our way down to the ferry slowly, past some big moth-eaten European bison, past the zebras standing stock-still as if the shadows of branches were cast upon them.

The Funeral

The telephone call came several days later. I heard Mom's low voice, and when she came into my room, I knew what had happened. "Söder?"

"Yes, he died last night. That was Nora calling."

"Was she—?"

"Very calm. The funeral will be next Sunday."

I rose up in my bed. "We'll go?"

"Yes. I think Nora would like it."

I lay there awhile longer, with my eyes closed. Images from summers long past, images of Söder, his face against the white pillows in the hospital, images of Nora at the zoo, when she felt uneasy and had to go—did she know then?

It was the last week of school, before the flowers were out. Things had calmed down, we had no more tests, the teachers read to us or let us do whatever we wanted; Rubberhead let those who wanted to walk go to the park and along the shore.

We got underway the following Sunday morning, all dressed up, Mom with a big bunch of flowers. It was raining slightly, narrow, purling beads of water slashed across the windowpanes. We were almost alone in the bus.

"Do you remember Grandfather's funeral at all?" Mom asked.

"Dimly. I sat in a car outside the cemetery. The chauffeur gave me candies."

"Nine years ago."

Mom looked out the window at the newly plowed fields, the long, narrow strip of forest. Sunlight was reflected in ditches. We passed a gigantic pile of wrecked automobiles, a red fence. Gradually the ramshackle houses thinned out, the forest took over, then suddenly stopped; nine twelve-story houses stood on a high, wide field like screens shielding each other. The forest around them had been cleared, three houses were placed facing the others. Some children were playing in the mounds of earth between the houses. A flame-colored bulldozer leaned its bucket with satisfaction against a pile of discarded lumber. The houses were painted green and blue. Balconies hung like baskets on the narrow, glinting rows of windows. A new whole city, it seemed to have shot up over a few days, like mushrooms.

"How can people live here!" Mom exclaimed.

"They can't, but they have to," Dad said.

"They have more light than Gerda and Marvin," I said.

"Yes, you're right. But all they have are dead fields around them and a long way into town."

We were silent. Smelling of gas and oil, the bus shuddered on down the narrowing roads. It drove through pine woods, the trunks straight and cool, an endless colonnade. Then the church appeared, white-walled, with the big boulder that was part of the wall and, across the road, the church bell tower that Nora's grandfather's great-great grandfather had built. We got out. Marvin was there, with Gerda; they had come down the previous day and stayed with Eskil. And Nora stood there. She was wearing a gray raincoat.

She hugged Dad and Mom, took my hand. She said,

"Thanks for coming. And please help bear the coffin, in the back on the right side."

As we walked toward the church door, the bells started ringing. They sounded so happy, so full, a rounded sound, not too eager, but almost proud.

Nora said, "I had nothing black to put on. For that matter, Söder wouldn't have liked it. You don't mourn with your clothes, he used to say. It's a shame to turn funerals into theater, he said. But I say that you can't avoid it completely."

She took off her raincoat. She was wearing a white blouse and a dark skirt.

"Well, we can begin."

People were already inside the church. The coffin was made of oak. Nora went and sat in the front pew. She smoothed her hand over her hair. People turned around. In the silence, a door closed. The organ began to play with a sigh. I looked at the old murals, my thoughts wandered. Silence fell, then a young priest spoke, very briefly. We got up when he sprin-kled the three handfuls of sand over the coffin. They clattered. He read a prayer. Then Nora walked forward, laid down her flowers quietly. They looked like field flowers, something blue, and daisies. No one said anything, nothing needed to be said. Old hunched men and women came. Some of the old women wore black kerchiefs. They went over to Nora and took her by the hand. Then we went over. I felt stiff. I looked at the coffin and tried to imagine Söder lying there. But it was unreal. The organ played, grew powerful, thundering like a storm. Its notes searched higher and higher, it piped and wound itself upward, then sank down again, died out in calm and stillness. Now the sky cleared, sun shone through the narrow windows, the flowers resting on the coffin brightened. Nora stepped forward, nodded to the bearers, who grabbed the straps. Nora was a bearer, too. She led the rest of us, straight and strong; slowly keeping pace, we carried the coffin to the grave. There was a wonderful scent of grass and spring. I, who had had to blink several times and look down in the church, suddenly felt how wide the field was, how high the sky. I took a deep breath of fresh air.

We slowly lowered the coffin, teetering around the rim, and drew up the straps. Nora fell to her knees and dropped in a little bunch of grape hyacinths. The lid was put on, and spruce boughs. People dispersed.

We stood awhile, then turned and went to the church door.

"There's not going to be any coffee after the funeral, because Söder didn't like that," said Nora. She squinted at the sun.

Marvin, who had sat like a poker throughout the funeral, and who had then stood by the coffin until Gerda virtually dragged him away, now opened his mouth for the first time.

"No, you don't drink coffee when you're dead."

"No," said Nora, "you don't. The locals and the old witches will bicker, but that's the way it's going to be. He never went to funeral parties himself. Now I'll be going. I'm not alone, I still have my aunt with me for a while, if I don't wear her out, or the other way around. When I don't want to be alone anymore, I'll get in touch. Now you should go see that your own plots are in order."

She hugged us, one by one. She said to Gerda,

"He had a good death. 'Feel my heart, how strangely it's beating,' he said. I felt how it fluttered, almost so you couldn't feel it. Then he just fell asleep."

She took a few steps, then turned. "The minister could have been worse."

She lifted her hand in farewell and walked hurriedly away. The iron gate squeaked shut.

We stood awhile by Grandfather and Grandmother's graves. There were fresh flowers, and light-green grass had shot up. Some jackdaws laughed in the cemetery wall. The food truck rattled past, empty. It was the summer food truck, the summer landscape, but everything was different. Marvin and Gerda were busy with Marvin's father's grave. Clouds drew shadows over the fields. A tractor drove past noisily, and the sun fell lower, shining right in our eyes.

The Catastrophe

A thundering of knocks sounded on Gerda's door. Matti, Gerda, and I were sitting talking at her round table. I was waiting for Marvin, who hadn't come back yet from the paper warehouse. It was a day of departure; everything felt strange, as if something completely new had entered my life.

It was the last day of school, and my report card felt like armor plate in my breast pocket. The next morning I would start as an errand boy in my father's office. Tomorrow I would begin my first working summer in the city. I felt I was changing my skin, or throwing myself out into the deep water, and I didn't really know if I could manage. Summer was here with flowers, with fun and pleasure, and—and the first money I would be earning myself!

Dad and Mom were still at work when I got home, and I couldn't stand being alone. I walked across the sun-warmed yard where the white lines of laundry slapped in the breeze from the balconies. I entered the warmth of the Lundgrens' apartment. Matti was smoking his pipe, sweet and mild.

Someone banged on Gerda's door so that it thundered.

I'd heard that knock before; I recognized it.

"Marvin!"

I dashed up and out into the vestibule. Marvin stood there, his face contorted, saliva dribbling from his mouth, his eyes almost lost in his face.

"She screamed! There! On the stairs! She lay in wait for me, trapped me! She's still got me!"

He stuttered, crumpled up. Gerda supported him, led him in. He half-lay on Gerda's bed, repeating monotonously in a broken, childlike voice, with his arms covering his eyes and head, "She screamed!"

"Tell us. Calm down. What happened?"

But it was as though he didn't hear us. Stammering, he stumbled on into another world where no voice could reach him, where he ran around, where he was afraid; he trembled. Gerda took a handkerchief and dried his mouth.

She said, "Marvin! Stop!"

He tossed his head back and forth, back and forth.

The doorbell rang; there wasn't a safe corner in the whole world, everything just went right on, as in a dream or nightmare.

"Come on in!"

Matti went out. We heard Mrs. Lehto's voice, screaming hoarsely, "Is he here? Is the madman here?"

Marvin pressed himself against the wall, his eyes distended with fear.

Gerda went toward her, barring her way. "What do you want?"

"He attacked my Ulla, and he'll answer for it! He ought to be in an institution! I'll report this! We can't have a madman in the house! The police ought to take a hand with him."

"Marvin has done nothing. He'd never do such a thing. There must be a misunderstanding."

"You only protect him. Look at him. He doesn't know what he's doing. He's a menace! But this is the end of his—his—I'll report him! He's insane! Insane!"

"Silence!" shouted Gerda, and silence fell. Mrs. Lehto's arms dropped to her sides. She took a step back, her face flushed and distorted.

"I know him, I'm his mother. He's done nothing, that's obvious. You just go report him and try to destroy him. You and all the others! Report him! Go ahead, leave us in peace! And ask your Ulla what really happened. As if you've asked her anything at all. I'll vouch for him! He's a part of my body, I know him, do you understand?"

She grabbed Mrs. Lehto's arm, but Mrs. Lehto broke away, shouting, "I've had it! This is it! Now you'll see!"

She ran out, slamming the door behind her. We were momentarily paralyzed.

We turned toward Marvin. He pressed himself against the wall, his face a white blotch against the dirty yellow wall.

"We have to get him to talk," said Matti. "If he can still . . ."

Gerda became absolutely silent. Her hands covered

Marvin's, which rested so helplessly on the embroidered bedspread. She turned slowly, "Do you believe
what she said? Do you really believe what she said?"

"We can't rule out the possibility, not entirely,
Gerda. Try to consider it realistically—"

He stopped. She stared at him. She looked at him
as if he were a stranger, someone slipping away, someone she no longer knew. Words were unnecessary. I
had to break the silence. I stammered out, "Never! He
could never have done that! I—I think I know
how—"

That was when the doorbell rang for the third
time. We turned toward the hall. Gerda rose,
exhausted, to go open it.

Just then Marvin rushed past us, saying, "No! They
mustn't get me!"

Before we were able to react, he had wrenched open
the door, escaped past Gerda, past Ulla and her
mother, half-weeping, tumbled out into the entry,
started running.

Then Matti hurtled after him, and, as I roused
myself, I heard Mrs. Lehto shriek, "It's all cleared up!
He wasn't the one. It wasn't—"

But it was too late. I don't remember any longer
how I found myself suddenly rounding the corner,
running down Sea Street, until I saw Matti about
thirty feet ahead of me, or how he veered at the corner, then turned off down toward the shore. I rushed
panting heavily after him, with only one thought in
my mind: "He'll get run over!"

An endless stream of cars rushed along the coast
road. Now and then the caravan stopped when a traf-

fic light turned red. The houses seemed to totter; people looked around; I ran. I was Marvin; I was no one; I cried out within myself, "No! Don't do it! Don't do it!"

Blindly, bewildered, Marvin threw himself out across the road, ran, made it by a hair's breadth in front of a car that braked violently. Matti gesticulated wildly, as if he wanted to stop the force of gravity. He actually got a car to stop, crossed over. The lights turned red. I ran as if my feet were stuck in tar, my burning lungs pressed upward into my throat; sunlight glittered on the ocean, the freshly painted boats, the smell of tar, gulls in flight, the last day of school; I ran, and meaningless words rattled in my head: Stop! Stop!

We ran out on the pier. Marvin turned. I could hardly see his face. He saw us coming. He was trapped. There was no way out. He ran back and forth on the farthest pier. Matti shouted,

"Marvin! Don't be scared! It wasn't you!"

And I shouted, "Marvin! Wait!"

He didn't hear us. We stopped. Matti took a few steps forward. "Marvin, come here! Everything will work out all right."

Gulls rose; somewhere a rising, falling, howling sound could be heard, an ambulance going somewhere. The sun stood high in the sky.

"Marvin!"

Suddenly Matti started to run toward him.

He saw Matti.

He took a step backward, let himself fall.

Matti
Says Good-bye

When you suddenly stop a film projector and the picture freezes, someone falling is caught in midair, and blurs; in this way, the image of Marvin falling burned itself into my retina and stayed there. He tried at the same time to protect himself with his arms and cried out for help, sharp, lamenting, like a sea gull.

The image is still with me, and since that moment, I've avoided talking superficially or scornfully about people who "do away with themselves" or do something "everyone" judges to be insane or crazy, about confused people, people we don't know but judge nevertheless, people we won't look at, push away from us, or perhaps lock up, people we try to hide or people we fight so hard that they are shattered forever. Marvin fell—he fell eternally.

"The life belt!" shouted Matti, rushing on, diving in. Suddenly everything meshed. I dashed to the stand, succeeded by muddling and pulling to get the life belt off its hook, ran with the belt and the line. I

heard people coming behind me. I threw it so hard
that my sight darkened. It nearly struck Matti on the
head. There was a splash, he battled with one arm; a
shadow slowly appeared, Marvin's face with his hair
plastered to his forehead. Holding him, Matti managed to get an arm over the life belt. Someone took
the line from my hand. I held fast, too. We pulled,
we hauled in toward the dock steps. They seemed
heavy as a stone. We got the line under Matti's arms,
hauled him up slowly. He heaved himself up onto
the pier in one motion, then grabbed and lifted Marvin. We laid him down on the pier. Water poured
off both of them, off all of us. Marvin opened his
eyes, didn't respond. Water ran out of his mouth. He
slowly turned on his side. Gerda was there, she knelt
down, laid her hand under his head. And Mrs. Lehto
was there.

I looked up at her and said, "He wasn't the one.
It was Peter who trapped him on the stairs, Peter who
had attacked Ulla already once before, and she didn't
dare tell you about it. She's scared of you, because
you're mean, because you scream a lot."

I tried to talk calmly. I realized that I sounded as
if my words came from a narrow funnel. My voice
shook and trembled. The whole world shook and
trembled. I didn't look at her. I watched Marvin's
face. It was lifeless, with lifeless eyes. He didn't say
a word. We managed to get him on his feet, supported
him; he let himself be led, saying nothing. No one
could reach him, he was far, far away. We hailed a
cab, which didn't want to take Matti and Marvin
because they were so wet, but Gerda shouted at the

driver. He opened the door, we put Marvin in, got him home, undressed, in bed. He tolerated us, didn't hear us. The doctor came. Marvin lay motionless in the kitchen alcove. I sat watching him, then sat awhile on the edge of Gerda's bed. Matti sat at the round table. The doctor talked in a low voice with Gerda in the kitchen. We were both silent. Matti had borrowed Gerda's bathrobe. He lit his pipe and said slowly, "I made a mistake. Do you think I can make it right again?"

"I don't know."

"He's in shock," said Gerda after the doctor had left. "I have to take care of him."

She talked as if to herself.

"Can I help?" Matti asked.

"You saved him," said Gerda. "That's enough. Now it's my turn. Now I take over, just me. You can tell them that I won't be at work. I'll take my summer vacation and then that's it."

"How will you manage?" Matti spoke doubtfully, seemed homeless.

"It'll work out. I still have something in the savings bank. Then we'll see. Marvin is all that matters now. Getting him back."

"It's also important for you to live."

She looked at him, but her eyes were somewhere else. She said, "There's a suit of yours in the closet, remember? You can take it now."

He said nothing, took the suit from the wardrobe, went into the bathroom.

Gerda stroked my hair, let her hand rest there a

second. Matti came out of the bathroom and said, "Where's my suitcase?"

"In the corner."

He took it, disappeared again. He came back; I got up.

Gerda put out her hand. "Thanks."

He took his suitcase. I followed him. He turned at the door. "Gerda, I'd like to come back."

"You're welcome," she said tersely.

The children were playing in the yard, some girls skipping rope. Someone called out, "Is he alive or dead?" but didn't wait for an answer.

We parted with a nod at my stairs. Matti went off, looking back swiftly. I sat down on the landing by the window. Out there was the hard backyard, every familiar inscription on the walls, every twist and turn of the drainpipe, every window. A murmur rose from the city; white laundry fluttered. It was my last day of school. Now came the summer; trees unfurled their fragrant leaves.

Even here in the yard, far from Paradise, from Bow Island.

Midsummer

On Midsummer Day we drove out to visit Marvin:
Gerda, Dad, Mom, and I. The two long, low, red
houses lay on a slope going down toward the bright
bay. Mentally handicapped children lived here, and
had a chance to learn a trade. They worked in the
garden or the carpentry shop, tirelessly, on that high
blue June day. They were on their knees, digging,
weeding, cleaning up, planting, completely absorbed
in their work, while hammering and the sharp noise
of a drill came from the shop. Three weeks had
passed since Marvin moved out here. It had taken a
long time for him to come to himself, back to us.

In the bus, Gerda explained, "He's been much
more peaceful this last week. He doesn't have his
bundle of fears any more. You'll see. But he's still
very quiet."

"And your own future?"

"I'm looking for a new job. Everything's still up
in the air. But it'll work out."

While the landscape sped past, memories also reeled

through my mind. Sometimes I didn't see the fields and woods; before me appeared Marvin's face, the smell of glue in the paper warehouse, or my own hands smelling of printer's ink from the office where I often sat stamping and sorting, when I wasn't sent out around the city. And people regimented in their glass offices, typing or going through papers or sending them on; writing and sorting, and Dad sat in one of the glass cages, talking on the telephone, writing and sorting. Buildings made of reports and papers. Days like copies of preceding ones. And the first payday, the first installment on a film camera with a zoom lens, so that I could take each shining butterfly, every remarkable insect, every flower I wanted to preserve, not dead in a herbarium but living, beautiful—and always there, on film. Or images from Söder's telescope, from the drainpipes in the backyard, metal roofs and balconies, from the city streets and the views out over the ocean, wide as the sky.

"You're too young to start working in the summer," Dad and Mom had said.

"You worked yourselves during the war, you always boast about that."

"That was different."

But I persevered and seemed to have developed broader shoulders from the effort.

I had to shade my eyes with my hand, but Marvin was nowhere to be seen.

"Come, I know where he is," said Gerda.

She walked quickly ahead of us toward the carpentry shop. Here, out in the woods and fields, it was as if she changed shape; here she was at home. It was as if a bit of Paradise, Bow Island, and summers past were here but at the same time very distant. Nora, Söder, who was still alive then, our own Pine Point, Erik and Beatrice—everything had changed, had to change. Perhaps Marvin had, too?

He was standing at one of the many workbenches, leaning forward, his hand slowly sliding along the edge of a cut plank. He felt it with his fingertips. The place smelled of fresh wood, a clean smell of forests, tar, and sawdust. Here and there were boys and girls busy drilling, planing, boring, or else sitting with pieces of wood in their laps, just holding them.

Marvin turned toward us, looked at us attentively, wrinkled his forehead. He lifted a piece of wood, offered it to us. It was a handle, smooth as skin, gracefully formed, a greeting. He hadn't varnished it, perhaps simply treated it with oil. You could see the gently waving pattern of the grain. I sniffed it: juniper, a scent of sun, warmth, summer.

"How great this is, Marvin! Did you make it?"

He nodded.

A woman wearing overalls came over. "Marvin does very good work. He has a knack with all kinds of woodwork, he gets it done without hurrying."

Dad said, "It really seems the only sensible thing— to work with pleasure, to be at peace or to work with others, the way you want to."

"It's not the only sensible thing, but it's a step in the right direction. Unfortunately, we can only take on a small number of those who need help."

Marvin felt along the edge of the plank with his thumb. He sighted along the plank, let the plane slowly glide forward, steadily; an even, spiral-shaped shaving curled down. Sunlight streamed in the window.

A door opened; rapid steps were heard. Marvin looked up, his face beamed; there was Nora, Nora with her round glasses, Nora with her arms raised:

"Hello there, all of you! Hello, Marvin! I thought I should come because I have important news. Important. But let's have a look first."

She examined Marvin's work, balancing and weighing the handle in her hand.

"It's good. We need a carpenter at home."

"We? At home? In Paradise?" Gerda asked.

"That's right. I'm quick, but I can't do it all alone. My aunt wants to go back to her home. The Bergströms at Norråker need a good carpenter who can help with their boat building. I've talked with them. And you'll live with me and housekeep and look after the cottage and everything while I go to my classes. What about it?"

Marvin had been listening. He slowly shook his head, slowly rocked his body, not confused, but marveling. He didn't understand.

"Home!" said Gerda. "Yes. Yes, that's how it has to be."

She hugged Nora, held her, saying, "Of course we'll come. Of course we'll come back. When Marvin . . ."

Nora interrupted her. "There's time. We can wait. But you can move in anytime you like. I've cleaned the rooms. And there's the fishing hut, too, for the three of you, this August. But it'll be a job to get it shipshape, I can tell you. So you can't be lazy. And you won't get it free. What about it?"

She pointed solemnly in turn to Dad, Mom, and me. "Nora! You're priceless!"

Nora and I danced around among the sawdust and shavings, a midsummer dance. Everything whirled around; my pounding heart somersaulted.

Out of breath, we leaned against a carpentry bench. Nora's glasses were crooked on her nose.

Marvin came over and gave Nora a wooden doorknob. He opened his mouth, searching; his lips searched, he leaned forward in his effort to speak. He managed to say, "Yours."

Then he turned abruptly and made his way back to his workbench, like a boat that takes a careful tack to test the wind and then turns back.

The June sun streamed in like a great joy.

Parting

~·~·~·

It was time to say good-bye.

We left Marvin there, in the warm carpentry shop. He didn't look around. Gerda stayed with him for a while. June clouds wandered with their shadows slowly over the earth. The teacher brushed her hair off her forehead and said,

"It's important not to give up. Here we realize that every beautiful thing helps a little on the way. A piece of wood, a flower, touching a sandpapered surface, creating something yourself, making something, seeing it slowly take form, become beautiful. This helps us keep going, because we're happy about it. Two steps forward, one step back. No, we don't forget the confusion or what isn't put into words, and we do fail. The thing that counts is not to hide anything away, above all, not them. We have to see that they are among us, part of us. Without difficulty, we wouldn't have any joy."

She offered us her firm handshake and then went

off. Gerda came out of the workshop, and we strolled toward the road. Walking beside me, Nora said,

"You'll come on the first of August."

"Yes, on the first bus."

"Good. You all look a little moth-eaten."

A boy came toward us, holding his big, heavy head at an angle. He had a bunch of flowers in his hand. He was trembling. Nora buried her nose in his bouquet and then announced, "It's lovely. It is really lovely!"

Still trembling, he smiled at her.

We stood by the side of the road, saying our goodbyes. Nora would go in one direction, the rest of us in the other. Our paths would cross soon again. Then, one day in the future, Marvin would board the bus with Gerda and return to Paradise.

"You don't know how happy you have made us, Nora," Mom said.

"Everything comes in its own time," said Nora. "And so it is."

With a swift gesture, she caught a bumblebee. We heard it mumble in her hand, then she opened her fingers and the bee vanished, invisible, against the wide sky.

The Author

Bo Carpelan is a well-known poet and novelist who lives in Finland and writes in both Finnish and Swedish. His children's books have won many prizes. *Bow Island* won the prestigious Nils Holgersson Plaque and the Finnish State Literary Prize. In 1973 he was on the Honor List for the Hans Christian Andersen Medal awarded by the International Board on Books for Young People. Mr. Carpelan, who was born in 1926, lives with his wife and two children in Helsinki.